SELF-WORTH

SELF-WORTH

EMMA THOLOZAN

TRANSLATED BY
EMMA RAMADAN

SCRIBE

Melbourne | London | Minneapolis

Scribe Publications
18–20 Edward St, Brunswick, Victoria 3056, Australia
2 John St, Clerkenwell, London, WC1N 2ES, United Kingdom
3754 Pleasant Ave, Suite 223w, Minneapolis, Minnesota 55409, USA

Originally published in French by Éditions Denoël
This edition published by arrangement with Éditions Denoël

Copyright © Emma Tholozan 2024
Translation copyright © Emma Ramadan 2026

All rights reserved. The publisher expressly prohibits the use of this book in connection with the development of any software program, including, without limitation, training a machine-learning or generative artificial intelligence (AI) system. Without limiting the rights under copyright reserved above, no part of this publication may be reproduced, stored in or introduced into a retrieval system, or transmitted, in any form or by any means without the prior written permission of the publisher.

The moral rights of the author and translator have been asserted.

This is a work of fiction. All of the characters, organisations, and events portrayed in this novel are either products of the author's imagination or are used fictitiously.

Typeset by Laura Thomas

Printed and bound in the UK by CPI Group (UK) Ltd, Croydon CR0 4YY

Scribe is committed to the sustainable use of natural resources and the use of paper products made responsibly from those resources.

978 1 761381 21 8 (Australian edition)
978 1 915590 97 8 (UK edition)
978 1 964992 38 9 (US edition)
978 1 761386 62 6 (ebook)

Catalogue records for this book are available from the National Library of Australia and the British Library.

scribepublications.com.au
scribepublications.co.uk
scribepublications.com

'[B]efore, they had had at least a passion for possessing.'

—Georges Perec, *Things: A Story of the Sixties*

1

I had been looking for a job. Or, rather, I had just found one. When my studies ended, so did my scholarship. As soon as I picked up my certificate, I headed for the employment office. Automatically. I followed the pack. Everyone knew this was a rite of passage after completing your master's.

I waited a few weeks for my next appointment. My eyes always glued to my phone. Ears pricked up in case it rang. The famous, liberating, even life-saving call! But my phone never rang. The screen stayed black. Finally, an employee contacted me. I had to go back to meet my new career counselor.

I woke up early so I could arrive at the office before it opened. Once there, I realized that many people had had the same idea. Great minds! The line stretched to the end of the street. The man behind me said to a friend: 'On my CV, I put "Facebook expert" to show that I know all about IT.

Good idea, right?' A restlessness streaked through the air. From time to time, someone stood on tiptoe, poked their head out over the others to see whether the metal shutters had finally been raised. It felt like we were outside a shopping mall on the first day of the sales. Maybe someone would even throw themselves at the doors. Taking greedy drags on our cigarettes and clutching the protective pouches holding our résumés, we wondered where all the full-time jobs were hiding. These days, you need an entire arsenal to have any hope of finding work. Photocopy of your ID, photocopy of your proof of residency, photocopy of your certificate of participation in Defense and Citizenship Day, photocopy of your diplomas. Dozens of pages just for the possibility of perhaps, the potential for maybe-I'll-get-lucky. All of us were clinging to this chance — too bad for the trees. The shutters opened suddenly, piercing the silence with their jammed mechanism; even they were tired. No one crawled under to be the first in the building, but we did jostle each other on the way in.

I grabbed a ticket. Number 56. Patience. Legs bouncing. Impatience. Several numbers were called, never mine. There was a whole gaggle of us. A farandole of the poor. We all adopted nearly the same demeanor, our gazes fixed on our canvas sneakers. Occasionally, we glanced at each other in silence, discreetly. How long has he been looking for a job? And that woman there, did she lose her eligibility for unemployment benefits? The level of experience could be measured primarily by the degree of the body's incline. The newbies seemed the most embarrassed. Backs hunched, folded in on themselves. Annoyed to be there. Over time, the spinal column straightens. Just because we're unemployed doesn't mean we shouldn't be proud. This is how you recognize the old-timers. Totally relaxed. They called the ladies at reception by their first names, asked about their children. But never exchanged words with the other job seekers. This was a tacit rule.

The room was full of posters featuring people who seemed very happy to work thirty-five hours a week for a miserable salary. I observed that display of optimism with a mix of disgust and hope. Number 56: it was my turn.

I met Marjorie, my new counselor. She introduced herself. She was there to help me. Together, we would succeed. She was a small woman and looked like a French bulldog, with big thick-lensed glasses and straight-cut hair. She was suffocating in her floral blouse: apparently, the air conditioning was broken, assuming it had worked at one point. Marjorie got straight to the point. We had to start my résumé over from scratch. I handed her the piece of paper that showed I had graduated with distinction. She turned it over several times. Her face crumpled. Dubious expression. 'Philosophy ...' She didn't finish her sentence. Since I was here, she deduced that I had decided against teaching. She asked me if I had any specific skills. I was a specialist in contemporary ontology, my 150-page thesis as proof. Also, I knew by heart the first ten axioms of Spinoza's *Ethics*. Slightly embarrassed, Marjorie checked the box for 'no special skills'. Her tap-taps on the keyboard became frenetic. She sighed, rubbed her glasses. Cleared her throat. She was firing on all cylinders, hunting for a job that required no skill. A Herculean task. Her fingers drummed away with impressive speed, a virtuoso, the clickety-clacks as sophisticated as a sonata. After several minutes of this performance, she sighed again, this time with satisfaction. Marjorie grabbed a Bic pen: 'Go tomorrow, at 9 am, to the address written here' — she handed me a page covered in assiduous handwriting — 'It won't be easy, but at least you'll be paid.' Then, she reeled off a slew of complicated words on the economic climate, including 'saturation of the job market', 'competitiveness', 'exponential productivity'. I could tell she wanted me to react, but the only reply I could muster was a Seneca quotation: 'It is not because things are difficult that we do not dare, it is because we do not dare that they are difficult.' Long silence. Followed immediately by shame. *Too nerdy*, I scolded myself. *Pretentious*. But Marjorie was pleased. Her eyes lit up with a gentle gleam. She asked me who had said that: an old man who was forced to slit his wrists.

I left the office without even looking at the paper Marjorie had given me. A little later, in the street, I unfolded it: 'audience warm-up'. A large gust of air blew between my ears; I had no clue what that meant. Whatever, I had a job. And anyway, there would be a trial period. I called my father to tell him the news. He was delighted. He wanted to know what the job was. When I told him I would be in charge of warming up the room, he expressed concern:

'It's not a porno, is it?'

'No, at least, I don't think so ...'

'Well, that's great! And you'll be paid?'

'Yes, I hope.'

'That's wonderful, Anna, bravo! Should we celebrate? I'll make crepes!'

He didn't leave me a choice: in the background, I could already hear him preparing the batter.

'And you, Papa, how's it going?'

'Same old ... So, what time will you be here? I can't wait.'

That night, Sophie was throwing a party. I didn't really know what we were celebrating. The end of something, probably. I didn't want to be in an apartment filled with a bunch of degenerates wearing black turtlenecks despite the 95-degree weather because they thought it lent them a sense of seriousness and credibility, everyone worked up by alcohol, wild from hormones, pupils dilated with happiness. All conversation would revolve around Plato, Kant, Deleuze, and French Theory. But I'd promised, so I went.

Dress. Lipstick. Metro. Buzz, stairwell, la bise. The heat was suffocating. End of July. Through the fumes of rum and the rings of smoke fogging up the room, I spotted Sophie's smile.

'About time! We were waiting for you.'

'Sorry, I was with my dad …'

'And you didn't bring us any crepes?'

A drop of sweat pearled on my forehead. I wiped it off with a paper towel and went to find myself a drink. I talked with the others. We had all done the same thing this week. 'Employment office' was on everybody's lips. Depressing. But, charmingly, we laughed about it. The elegance of despair. And the solidarity of hopelessness. We patted each other's shoulders. We offered what little comfort we could. Brothers and sisters of those back-breaking school benches. Spending three hours per week trying to understand the disjunctive syntheses had given us the illusion that we were a family. So, like a family, we wanted to hear each other's news. Élodie had registered on a babysitting site; Mehdi had an interview for a job in a fast-food restaurant.

'Aren't you a communist?'

'Well, everybody's gotta eat.'

Touché. For all of us, the horizon was full of odd jobs, but we didn't mind. Philosophy had taught us to disdain material possessions. Each year, for my birthday, my father racked his brain. A nice watch? A new pair of shoes? No, Papa, you know I don't need any of that. Give me books,

books, and more books. It's more pure. Anything to avoid becoming a slave to Big Business! We delighted in the magnanimity of our souls, even if it meant flipping burgers on a griddle. I said nothing about my new job. I didn't talk about the prospect of warming up a studio audience. Modesty comes easily to me; optimism is more difficult. I preferred to listen. Between two drinks, Sophie pulled me aside.

'So, Anna, do you think you can help me study for the CAPES? Recite the lessons with me, all that?'

She was overflowing with enthusiasm, like a little girl starting elementary school. I felt it was my duty to warn her.

'Are you sure that's a good idea? You'll be sent to who knows where in France. You'll have horrible hours with a ton of work to grade every week. Apparently, sometimes, they even pay you three months late.'

'You're such a cynic. What about the joy of passing on knowledge? Have you thought about that? The happiness of seeing highschoolers blossom? And besides, I don't know what else to do ...'

I thought of the Malraux saying: 'Friendship is not about being with your friends when they are right, it's about being with them even when they are wrong.' If Sophie wanted to crash into a wall, I would press on the accelerator with her. I said, 'Okay, if that's what you want, we'll start as soon as I get settled at work!' Sophie must have sensed that

I wasn't exactly thrilled, so she extended her pinky in the air for me to hook onto (she knew that always softened me), and the pact was sealed.

Meanwhile, the muggy ambiance turned heavy. A thick lid had come down on the pressure cooker of our lives, the windows were coated in a dense mist: I was simmering.

When the conversation became too oppressive, I started to dance. It began with a spasm. Ridiculous. A slight bending of the legs, more or less to the rhythm. More less than more, in fact. Soon, with the help of the alcohol, my arms joined in. Twitchy movements and big circles. Alternating. Hips opening after being stiff for too long. I closed my eyes and batted my lashes, shook my head. I was trying to be sensual, but I probably looked like a maggot on a hook. I wasn't dancing, I was flailing. The femininity of fashion magazines was nowhere in sight, no Axelle Red either. The speakers kept pumping out catchy songs, rap and pop, French and American. We pretended to know the words, we lip synced. Then the music slowed.

As expected, the conversation soared into the sky of ideas. Grand notions, love, liberty, death. Words chewed over again a thousand times in different mouths; it was like listening to a broken record. The same nursery rhyme on loop since antiquity; if we'd been wearing togas it would have made no difference. I felt sick. We had been sold the concept of the philosopher king, a prominent place in society, but Plato had it all wrong. You can explain the nuance between justice and equity? That's great, but we need someone to stock the shelves, so that won't help. Next! A furry feeling carpeted my tongue. I downed one cup after another of bad alcohol, pretending to be interested in the discussion. Chin nod. Prudent pout. Pursed lips.

That's when he drove his two emeralds straight into my irises. I saw him straight away, even from afar. In the middle of that absurd galaxy, I saw him straight away. He became the center. Beautiful as the sun. A white face framed by jet-black hair. High cheekbones beneath haunting green eyes, nearly translucent. The kind you only see in Photoshop. He had a face made for film, but I couldn't pinpoint what genre. He was telling a story about a line at a cash register. The girl opposite him was roaring with laughter. She tilted her head back, then fixed her bangs with a falsely careless gesture. Dazzling blonde. A shampoo ad.

The guy's voice didn't manage to drown out the Sting song Sophie had put on in the background. So I could hear, in snippets, the starts of his jokes, without the punchlines, but I was hooked anyway. A disco ball studded his face with silver spots. The luminous specks danced a three-step waltz, yellow, violet, and pink. Everything solidified at once. My blood wasn't flowing properly, it suddenly seemed very thick. My heart stopped for a moment.

After sitting on the couch, he signaled for me to come over. The force of my attraction was intense, but I was completely wasted. It took all my energy to put one foot in front of the other without stumbling. Total concentration. *Go on, Anna, you can do it. Left, then right. Right, then left, that's it.* I had a terrible stomachache and my vision was blurry. I collapsed next to him as if I hadn't sat down in ages. He asked whether I was more into continental or analytic philosophy. I stared at him suspiciously. I'd had my fair share of handsome, brooding, Nietzsche-citing types while I was in school. 'I'm teasing you. The two of us don't give a shit about all that, am I right?' Yeah, we don't give a shit about all that.

I was surprised I hadn't crossed paths with him at the university. This made sense, since he hadn't gone to school there. He repaired things. That's how he'd met Sophie — through a friend of a friend who knew him. She was having problems with her computer. Since she was a broke student, to repay him, she had invited him to her party. Immediately I glanced at his hands. Reflex. Brainiac instinct. They were calloused. Sturdy. A few scratches. Fingers that did something other than hold a pen to write a thesis. He noticed I was staring, and squeezed his fist so hard between his thighs that his knuckles turned white. I was embarrassed. I tried to make a joke.

'Descartes enters a bar. The guy behind the counter says to him: "Would you like something?" He responds: "I don't think —" and then, he disappears.'

Wow. Five years of school for that. It was total crap, and yet I'd put everything I had into that little witticism. I panicked. I don't think he got it, but it worked, he smiled. My heart stopped for a second time. Then I noticed the small dimple on his right cheek. I'm sure it was on the right because we were sitting side by side. It looked like a comma. It suited him, that comma, because his words poured out in a continuous surge, with no period. No pause between his stories, one right after the other with a disconcerting effortlessness.

'I know some bad jokes, too. You want to hear one? What's the difference between a dollar and a rouble?'

'I don't know.'

'A dollar!'

This time I was the one who didn't get it, but I drank in his words, I laughed at everything he said. White teeth, neck thrown backwards. Suddenly, I remembered the other girl, the shampoo ad one, and then I kept my head still. We talked, and I felt my stomach tighten. An invisible hand was twisting my guts. Cramps. Gurglings. Reflux. Such grace. He wanted to hear what I was going to do with my life, if I was okay talking about it, maybe it wasn't the time or the place, maybe I'd rather rejoin the others? And then, I vomited. On his shoes. A pink, fizzy substance: strawberry gin and tonic, rookie mistake.

He wasn't upset at all, quite the contrary. He laughed again. Thunderously this time. He was clutching his sides while shaking his foot over the rug. The blonde girl threw me a smug look. He stood up, took me by the hand, and murmured in my ear: 'I think it's time to go to bed.' And so we took off, leaving the Kantians in our wake.

The street had changed texture. The building facades looked comfortable; I wanted to lean against them. The ground no longer exhaled the heat stored up from the day before. Gone, the steaming tar and the plastic soles sticking to it. The air had cooled down. It was easier to breathe. In the distance, a young dawn was quietly awakening, tinging the roofs with orange hues. I looked at his watch, resting with his forearm on my shoulder. I had to be up in three hours. He didn't speak. I didn't either. But it was nice. An enveloping sensation with each stride. The clicking of his boots on the pavement set the tempo of our walk. We bumbled along. Arm in arm. He wore my bag on his back. I wore my heart on my sleeve. We passed only the garbage collectors and old insomniacs out walking their dogs. There was tenderness in their gazes. I clung to my companion like a mussel to its rock. Unsteady steps. Zigzagging path. What did they think of us?

Eventually, I recognized my street. The familiarity did me good. An anchor point in this city that seemed to be spinning around me. Everything in sight swaying. I was able to collect my thoughts. When we arrived at my front door, I hesitated before entering the code, my finger hovering in the air. Suspense. 3948. No. 9348. No. Third time's the charm. I didn't think to invite him upstairs. I muttered a fetid-breathed thank you. He waited until I was in my apartment, and even a little longer. When I went to draw the curtains to sleep, he was still there, outside, standing, serene. I waved at him from the window. I saw his silhouette cross to the other side of the street, sink into the ochre rays of light and disappear completely. The light had swallowed him up.

2

The alarm blared like an insult. Eyelids cemented shut, I could barely get up. The previous night hit me with full force. Physically. Headache, temples pounding, dizziness. It felt like my head was in a bag that a kid was gleefully slamming against a wall. I had to do damage control. Glass of water. Doliprane. Quickly brush my teeth. My brown hair was staticky and stuck to my cheek, which was still covered in drool. In front of the mirror, memories started to rush back in fragments. I thought of him and his ruined hands, frustrated at not being able to remember what we had said to each other. What I had said to him, especially. But there was no time to think. *Quickly, put on a T-shirt. Proper attire, what does that mean?*

My mouth still furry, I took the metro, then another metro, then the RER. Would it never end? I clutched the address that I had scribbled on a piece of paper in case my phone ran out of battery. I also had the kind letter of recommendation from Marjorie. The Doliprane was starting to kick in. I wasn't feeling too awful. I had left my headphones on the bedside table, so I listened only to the strident sound of the train as it stopped, started again, stopped again. Unhappy travelers entered, crammed together. Stench of sweat, no one looking at each other. At certain stations, the crowd unloaded in dribs and drabs, while at others, a powerful surge tumbled out. Tonneau des Danaïdes: even more travelers. Dreary rain on the platform. I had finally arrived.

The rest of my route was like a science-fiction movie. I had to walk quite some way and traverse a no man's land where a bunch of gigantic hangars had been dumped. All gray and evidently deserted. Except that as I neared, I could see that things were happening inside. Little cars, like those the bourgeois drive on a golf course, but these people didn't seem rich. Dressed in black, they were covered in wires going in every direction. Headset with a microphone, walkie-talkie, and cables, loads of cables. I couldn't decipher their strange ballet, a frantic race from one hangar to another. Amidst this bustle, I noticed lines of people. Immense, immobile queues. Fathers and mothers, prepubescent tweens, young girls wearing too much makeup. They had come in packs, groups of girlfriends, in couples, or alone. I skirted these hordes, dodging the golf carts and the women in evening gowns.

I was supposed to go to building A. Making my way through this mysterious jungle, I eventually found it. When I cut the line, people started to complain. I shrugged my shoulders by way of apology. The hangar's metal door was shut and completely solid. The kind of door that would give a burglar second thoughts. The kind of door you don't enter without an invitation. So I knocked. Three discreet, almost apologetic taps. Then I waited. After a few seconds, I knocked again, harder this time. The enormous metallic panel traced a semicircle, the hinges squeaked, and a completely unremarkable man appeared in the opening. I was disappointed: neither druid nor giant, he too was dressed in black; he too was wearing a headset, walkie-talkie, and wires that hung from every part of his body. He signaled for me to come in and brusquely closed the door behind me.

'You're late, on your first day, not a good look,' he snapped.

I made excuses — I had been waiting behind the door for a while, he hadn't heard me.

'You mustn't wait for doors to open! You must break them down.'

I wondered where he'd heard such a phrase. It reminded me of the inspirational quotes printed on calendars, the wrappers of Christmas chocolates, or teabags. Then I thought of Marjorie; she would have appreciated this maxim. The man introduced himself: Marc.

'I'm Anna.'

'Okay, that's irrelevant.'

I waved the letter from the employment office in his face, but he didn't even glance at it.

'You're replacing Mélanie. She burned out or something. In my opinion, she was just lazy. Where were you before?'

I told him that I had studied philosophy. He replied, 'Good grief.'

I followed him down a hallway that led to another huge door. This one was open. I felt a moment of relief. We entered an enormous room being used as the set. The high ceiling was impressive, but I didn't notice it right away. First, Marc led me to a group of people, his cable comrades. He pointed at each of them and listed their names and jobs. I forgot everything immediately. Then Marc left me in the care of Sandrine, a small brunette with a short dress and a luxury handbag who, before saying hello, stared at my worn-out shoes.

'I thought sneakers would be better for walking.'

'Yes, better for walking, my thoughts exactly ...'

I would be working with her, but she was in desperate need of coffee, she was ready to drop. She would be back in a few minutes. Carnivorous smile. Hand on her hip. Hair swish followed by the aroma of expensive perfume. That's when I looked up.

Attached to the ceiling, men in black clothing were

flying around. Like modern-day angels, on seats suspended from thick metal beams and filming from a high angle. To get up there, they climbed a ladder with very thin rungs, accompanied by lighting engineers who pointed spotlights from either side. It was busy on the ground, too. Dozens of little hands plugging in equipment, synchronizing the teleprompter. Some cleaning the rows of chairs or vacuuming. Opposite me was the stage with its giant screen and colorful decorations. It was a popular music competition show that my father and I used to watch on Saturday nights. The excessive brightness of the projectors burned my retinas. They were doing soundcheck. One-two. One-two. I was very intimidated. I had no idea why I'd been sent here.

Sandrine returned at last. With a cup of boiling coffee in her hands and dark circles under her eyes, she seemed exhausted by a day that hadn't even begun. I felt a surge of pity.

'It's always like this, there are too many things to do and not enough time, we just try to stay afloat, we run around all over the place. I'm the crowd coordinator. Basically, when the audience arrives, I place them. You'll see what I mean in a minute. And you, your task is to warm them up. You have to channel a good mindset, be full of happiness.'

She continued on like this, making liberal use of English vocabulary. In fact, my job consisted mainly of telling the audience when they should applaud (constantly), and when they should laugh (also constantly). Clap clap, Sandrine dutifully showed me with her hands, in case I didn't know what the word 'applause' meant.

The people who'd been lined up outside started flooding the set. Sandrine immediately took charge. A true maestro. She made sweeping gestures designating precise placements. You, here. You, over there. It seemed arbitrary, and at the same time Sandrine seemed to know exactly what she was doing. On the lookout for anyone trying to change their seat, she glared like a hawk. No unauthorized movement. Two middle-aged women complained: 'This is the third time we've come and we're always in the back, we waited four hours outside. We want to see Bertrand too!' Sandrine responded kindly but firmly. Her only explanation: that's just how it is. Bertrand was the show's host, an old man with a fluorescent-orange complexion whom all my new colleagues venerated wholeheartedly: a nice illustration of Stockholm Syndrome.

Sandrine had alluded to avoiding a shipwreck, but what happened on set was nothing like a cruise ship. Here, women and children didn't come first. When all the seats were taken, the truth struck me in the face. As skillful as a surgeon, Sandrine had traced the contours of the crowd with her scalpel, blending traditional aesthetic ideals and ruthless capitalist logic. She had placed the young and beautiful in the front, the old and ugly in the back, as simple as that. She knew where the cameras panned. First and second rows. Seat 37 on the right side, 54 and 73 on the left. In each of these seats, there needed to be a harmonious face. She let the lighting engineers do their work, casting shadows over the fat and disabled. The renegades, the downgraded of this free audience. Of course, the guinea pigs themselves were unaware. Sandrine was clever and warm enough to give everyone the impression that they had a part to play. That they were all on equal footing. That they were the stars, even. The complaints were slowly drowned out by the jingle test runs. Sandrine returned satisfied. Mission accomplished. She turned towards me and handed me the headset: I had to crouch down under a camera. Over the backdrop of the audience's clamors, the members of the jury came in and sat down one by one in their large chairs and then, a few seconds later, Bertrand walked onto set: Mass could begin.

I must have looked like a rabbit caught in headlights. I was lost. Without any preparation, I'd passed to the other side of the screen, in a strange third dimension where everyone was cooing 'ma chérie' and 'mon chou', even those who didn't know each other. The show fashioned itself a springboard for young artists. Singers of all genres. Multicolored outfits. Hoarse voices. Vibrato. I had trouble masking my disappointment. It was less impressive in real life. The decor was cheap, a kind of wobbly PVC. The live format diminished the charisma of the contestants: after being used to seeing them well-lit and closeup, I found them much smaller in person. Their voices often trembled. The shock mounts would fix these flaws. Between appearances, Bertrand went back into makeup. They repowdered his nose, smoothed his complexion. Meanwhile, expressionless, he tapped away on his cellphone. He didn't listen to any of the music, but each time he came back on stage, eyes riveted to the teleprompter, he addressed the contestants with a flash of benevolent wit. In any event, he couldn't hear anything, and the audience couldn't either, because the speakers weren't facing us.

I was on autopilot. Outside of my body. 'Your arms, not your head, Anna,' Sandrine whispered to me. 'Or actually, yes, you need to learn to think *with* your arms.' They had quickly shown me the different gestures I had to reproduce. Stimuli and response to stimuli, like training a dog, and just as trivial. I gave the crowd the signal for applause. Docile, they complied. It was an audience of regulars. Responsive. Some showed off and yelled a lot. The host just had to say something like 'So, not bad, huh?' and I would make the gesture for laughter. My protégés cracked up. Full-throated. Mouths agape. It went on like this for an hour and a half. I listened to the different tonalities of these laughs. Sometimes high pitched, sometimes deep. Always forced. But no matter, from afar it was believable. That was the important thing. Together, we created the illusion of a world that weeps with joy, as if no misfortune could ever penetrate the sheet metal of this hangar. Tragedies, sadness, wars, and catastrophes couldn't pass through these gray walls, crowned with divine protection. An eternal happiness.

When I let more than three minutes go by without universal guffaws, someone tapped me on the back to remind me of my task. Raise the arms, lower them again. I was Charlie Chaplin, but I didn't know if this was *Modern Times* or *The Great Dictator*. I was exhausted; I felt like I'd gone through the spin cycle of a washing machine. When a contestant was eliminated, the lights were finally turned off, and the audience stood. I gathered my things to leave. Implacable, Sandrine grabbed me by the collar: 'Where do you think you're going? We have another episode to shoot.' Not even time for a cigarette or a sandwich. Another batch of impatient people to seat. Another round of protests. Another explanation yelled into the microphone: 'This gesture means applaud'; 'This one means laugh'. My arms started to ache. My gaze flickered. My eardrums were about to implode. We filmed four episodes in a row.

At 6 pm, the hangar door closed behind me. I could finally leave. I welcomed the return trip of two metros and the RER with joy and gratitude. I noticed the same passengers as on the way there, their jackets now crumpled and their ties undone, but their faces still pale. I looked for an empty seat, I needed to sit down and close my eyes. My legs were cotton. I didn't want to be jostled, I just wanted to collapse on my bed. I didn't think of *The Society of the Spectacle*, of Debord or the others. I was too wrecked to think. Sitting at the other end of the same train car, Sandrine had taken off her pumps to stick a Band-Aid on her sore heel. Like my colleague, I had one priority: take care of my suffering body. I was so tired that my dark circles had dark circles.

A senior executive was speaking loudly to another senior executive. I almost told them to talk more quietly, but I didn't have the energy. Instead, I turned my phone back on and found a message from my dad. He wanted to know how my first day had gone. I was touched. At the same time, I felt a lump materialize in my throat. That lump, I knew it well. It wasn't there when I was little; it came later. The first time it appeared was on the middle school playground. My girlfriends were blowing big chewing-gum bubbles under the plane trees greened by spring. Adam Lesieur was sitting on a bench. Blond curls, silver braces, and a cool skateboard. I was in love, terribly in love. I couldn't take my eyes off his lips. I dreamed of slipping my hand into his. One day, I decided to tell him everything I was feeling in a letter. I put it in his locker and hid, restless, so that I could watch him find it. He opened his locker, and the little white envelope fell to the floor. He broke the seal, creased his eyes to read it carefully, and that's when tragedy struck. Tapping his best friend on the shoulder, he laughed. Sincerely laughed. An eruption. Almost like gargling.

Within an inch of a trance. The earth trembled beneath my feet. After scanning his surroundings, he charged at me, the letter half crumpled in his right hand, the skateboard under his left elbow.

'What's your name again? Anna the freak? Come on, look at you, you're so ugly, you're always wearing the same clothes, plus you're dyslexic, there are so many spelling errors in this thing. How could you think I'd be interested in you? You're a nobody.'

And then he'd skated over to the less ugly girls whose dictation grades were better than mine. I went back home, devastated, and curled into the fetal position under the covers. My father asked me what had happened.

'Do you think I'm ugly?'

'You're in a tough stage of life, Anna, but things will get better soon, I promise. To me, you're already perfect. Alright, come on, I'm making you crepes.'

That had comforted me for about a second and a half, but at least he'd tried. Once I'd eaten my snack, back in my bedroom, I scrutinized myself in the mirror. I had to admit that my head wasn't very symmetrical, and my eyes seemed disproportionate in comparison to the rest of my face. As for my ugliness, so be it, I couldn't do anything about it, but my spelling was another matter. I wasn't going to settle for devouring the dictionary and the Bescherelle, no. I was going to be an intellectual, even if my father switched the channel whenever writers or philosophers were on TV because he preferred to be entertained. I was sure that in the Lesieur family, things were different. They probably watched *C dans l'air* and France Culture, listened thoughtfully to each guest and discussed their words over dinner, because those people, they were listened to, they were respected. What they said mattered. Adam would never have asked them where their clothes were from, what their parents did for a living, or what neighborhood they lived in. So, I made up my mind: I would become someone.

That was the plan. But despite my determination, the big lump of Adam's words never disappeared. It came back in moments of sadness, in the depths of fatigue and anguish. That day, in the packed RER train car, it kept me from swallowing.

I tried to ignore it. I took a deep breath full of train-car stenches and typed a reply to my father: 'Great, I'll tell you all about it.' He must have been glued to his phone, because a second later I received two ecstatic smiley faces and a thumbs up. Could have been worse.

I emerged from the metro. The walk back had never seemed so long. Halfway home, my knees buckled. My pulse raced more than usual. The guy from the night before was standing in front of my door. He was waiting with his foot against the wall, as if to prop it up. I panicked. The closer I got, the more precisely he took shape. Silhouette first, then his face. He was handsome, just like in my half-memory. As I approached him, I stammered, trying to remain as casual as possible:

'Oh hey, what are you doing here?'

'I wanted to see you again.'

'Have you been waiting here all day?'

He assured me no, that he had just arrived. Obviously, he was lying. I could tell by a cute giveaway, an inflection of the voice, a slight hesitation at the start of the sentence. I felt my cheeks turn red; I lowered my eyes. At his feet, the ground was littered with a heap of cigarette butts, the same brand he was now smoking. So, he'd been loitering here all day, or at least a good part of it.

We stayed planted in front of each other without saying a word. Arms dangling, mouth beginning to form a syllable, then renouncing. Finally, I offered him a tour. He followed me into the labyrinth of my neighborhood and asked me how my first day had gone. I must have had a strange expression on my face, because he immediately followed up with 'I wasn't spying on you — you told me about it yesterday.' I had no memory of this. I wanted to answer something along the lines of what I had said to my father, but opposite his sincere gaze, I felt forced to be sincere, too. Everything poured out. A revolting surge of jagged words. I told him about the commute, the door, Sandrine, my aching arms. I described the fake paradise, the simulated happiness. The more I spoke, the more the lump in my throat grew.

Soon it took up all the space, and the story couldn't come out. I stopped talking. He simply nodded.

After a few suspenseful moments, we resumed our walk. Our arms drifted towards each other in an involuntary motion. The attraction was still there, as strong as the night before. Electric skin. When we grazed each other, we had to get a hold of ourselves. A shiver ran through me, and I tried to keep my arm straight along my body. It worked for a minute, then off it went again. Our tiny skin cells wanted to meet.

I needed to sit down somewhere; I was so tired. We stopped at the supermarket to buy a bottle of red wine. We walked up the stairs. The five floors. Key in the lock. We were at my place.

His gaze darted everywhere. Through his eyes, I saw the dishes piled up in the sink, the dirty underwear thrown blindly on the floor, and the dust, not only in the corners that the vacuum never managed to reach, but absolutely everywhere. I disgusted myself. I almost never had people over, and I had gotten used to my own filth. But he only commented on the large movie poster — *La Ruée vers l'or*, a film he loved.

I went into the kitchen to open the bottle of wine. From the living room, he told me jokes. As at Sophie's party, his words were interrupted by the sound of silverware. In response to the racket I was making, ransacking the drawers in search of a corkscrew, he offered his help. He entered the cramped room. I felt his warm breath on my neck. My back tensed involuntarily. I turned around, the precious tool in hand and a certain pride in my gaze. He took my arm, and the rest of my body followed. It was on. Our pelvises touched. I dropped the corkscrew. Our heads drew closer. Our bodies squeezed together. His face so close to mine. Broken into pieces, shattered as in a kaleidoscope. Eyebrow. Ear. Neck. Chin. Then, our mouths collided. Forgotten, the kisses of teenagers. This was a true melding of fluids and tongues. Mounting endorphins, exploding dopamine. Euphoria. Taste buds ecstatic to savor the other. Cheeks ablaze. Rapidly, we changed course. We crashed into the bedroom furniture because, out of modesty, he didn't want to turn on the lights. The sounds of the city were muffled by the walls and, inside, a new murmur. His trembling breath, small sigh. My hand, his back. His kisses, my shoulders. I'd had sex before. But this was different. Neither better nor worse, just different. He was aerial, light. He didn't put all his weight on me like the others. I wanted it to last even longer. I watched his throat swell, his hands graze my hips. Finally, he turned toward me. I kissed him again. In the dark, his eyes were fluorescent.

I got up to grab the bottle and two glasses. Back wedged against the wall, he let the ashtray rest on his stomach, and we smoked. We had spoken plenty before and during, but now we had to fill up the after. This was always the most difficult part. I wanted to start a sentence with his name, to tell him how good it was, but I realized that I couldn't remember his name. I spent some time trying to recall the people who'd been at the party. I recited the alphabet, stopping at each letter to see if it rang any bells. It was too late, impossible to ask him now. He made a point of saying 'Anna', as if assuring himself that he was really with me. He read my thoughts.

'Charles-Lucien.'

I thought it was another one of his silly jokes, so I burst into uncontrollable laughter. I spit wine into his face. The red droplets that flecked his skin contrasted with his disproportionate seriousness: he wasn't laughing.

'That's my real name.'

'Ah,' I replied. 'Can I call you Lulu?'

'Like Beckett's prostitute?'

We talked, drank, and smoked for a long time. We talked about everything and anything. Our respective lives, our families, our childhoods — we needed to know every detail about each other.

'If you enjoyed high school, why didn't you go to college after?'

'My parents were full on. For my mom, I had to be a minister or something, nothing less. But that wasn't for me. I've never believed in meritocracy.'

As it happens, I found him quite intelligent, much more than me.

'And I wanted to do something useful. Well, I mean,

really useful, not be shut inside an office all day.'

He spoke nonstop, but in a whisper, so as not to exacerbate the tinnitus I'd brought home from work as a little welcome gift. The idea of going back there the next day made me want to defenestrate myself. I followed the incandescent end of his cigarette as it whirled from place to place. It traced enigmatic, evanescent shapes. An indoor firework. I fell asleep without realizing it, the taste of ash in my mouth. I dreamt of Sandrine and Bertrand, and of Lulu too, I think. When I woke up, he was already gone, but he'd left his phone number and some earplugs on the nightstand.

3

Lulu and I saw each other again several times. It got to the point that we never really parted, to tell the truth. And then he moved in with me. When I suggested it to him, I hadn't even finished my sentence before he was already saying 'yes yes yes', his pupils huge, like his arms. He enveloped me in them.

The day he was supposed to move into my apartment, I was waiting for him near the window, my eyes scanning the street. Would he arrive on a truck? Would all of his things fit in the apartment? Twenty-five square meters isn't very big. I'd been so excited that the logistical details had gone six miles over my head. Lulu was two hours late. Finally, I spotted him running in the middle of the street, all alone, like an imbecile. He was oozing happiness. Practically jumping for joy. He waved at me wildly and nearly fell over. I watched the street behind him to see if there was a car in his wake. To my great surprise, he had only a big box under one arm and an object I couldn't identify under the other. He raced up the five floors, I could hear his heavy steps in the stairwell. He arrived breathless, threw the box on the ground and hid his right hand behind his back. Then he brandished it before me suddenly, revealing a bird cage.

'TA-DA! It's my gift for our apartment. What do you think? Pretty cool, huh? Two lovebirds. I find them so beautiful, don't you? At first, I wanted to get a dog, but then I realized that wouldn't be very practical. The birds are better, right?'

He was talking a mile a minute, the little comma on his right cheek jumping up and down.

'What should we call them?'

'Great question! Well, Anna, let's think.'

He put the cage in the living room and wiped his sweat with the back of his sleeve.

'If I'm Lulu, then that would make them Vladimir and Estragon. Look, it's like they're always watching for something. Heads tilted to one side, then the other. They're waiting for Godot.'

'But what if one of them is female?' I ventured.

'Don't be such a square, little love! Female, male, who cares.'

Meanwhile, I'd finished my probationary period at work. Marjorie called me one night. She was all fired up, practically screaming on the phone. 'They're keeping you on, they're keeping you on!' I felt like I was one of those old dogs from La Société Protectrice des Animaux whose owners can bring them back if they're too mean. The show's HR department had told her that I wasn't exactly a ray of sunshine, but that I did my job properly, so I could stay. Marjorie was in such a frenzy and used so many superlatives that she nearly convinced me I'd scored an incredible job.

To thank her, I invited her to come watch an episode on set. She took a day of leave or called in sick, I don't remember. The day of the recording, I saw her in the crowd, without her glasses, which had been swapped for contact lenses. She was wearing a pretty dress, the kind you stop and look at in a store window. Marjorie hadn't wanted to embarrass me. She was delighted when I told her she wouldn't have to wait in the line. She walked in ahead of the others, haughty, very proud. Sandrine sat her at the back of the room, but Marjorie didn't mind. She kept giving me an enthusiastic thumbs up. As soon as I signaled to the audience, she performed the gesture with grace. At the end, Marjorie came to see me. We shared a soda while she spiritedly rehashed the episode. An instant replay. She laid it on thick, marveling at the ambiance. I knew that she was going to recount the story to her girlfriends at the employment office the next morning, and this made me happy.

I had already received my first paycheck. When the deposit arrived in my account, Lulu and I were over the moon. Minimum wage wasn't amazing, but it was still something. A celebration was in order. We didn't even think to go to a restaurant. We ate at the fast-food place where Mehdi worked. Busy behind the fryer, he accidentally burned himself when he noticed us. Quickly, he went to the register to take our order. It was a celebration. XXL menu and fries all around. He gave us a discount, even though he wasn't allowed. It was the beginning of September, and the cold had started to petrify the city. Lulu and I were shivering a little in our sweaters; Mehdi was sweating under his baseball cap. He congratulated me on landing a job. That's when a manager realized Mehdi was taking an unauthorized break and pounced on him.

'You're not getting paid to shoot the shit.'

'You're right. I'm supposed to cook the shit, not shoot it.'

I was pretty impressed by his comeback. The manager continued on his way without turning back around. Mehdi breathed out between his teeth and said that he was going to quit soon anyway because working there was too depressing, and he was dying of heat all day long.

We devoured our burgers under his benevolent gaze. Lulu caressed my arm with devotion, as if I had accomplished something extraordinary. He licked his fingers. On the booths shiny with grease, eating our desserts, we made big plans. We were already imagining the house we would buy and the amazing countries we'd travel to on vacation. The adult life that people dreamt of took shape before our eyes. We were well aware that with my salary, we weren't anywhere close to owning a house. But that didn't matter. Outside, the stars were winking at us.

Besides, Lulu also worked — very hard, in fact. He repaired a motley heap of thingamajigs. He was a resourceful entrepreneur. In the morning, after finishing his coffee, he put on classical music, and I watched his big hands get to work. Pliers. Mozart. Screwdriver. Schubert. Drill. Beethoven. Sander. Mahler. A full arsenal. Lulu didn't have a specialty. He was a jack of all trades. No machine could resist him. Sometimes, he brought back an object that had no identifying features. Unrecognizable. I'd go shower and when I returned, I'd see that it was a toaster. Good as new. Our apartment soon housed an astronomical number of objects. They accumulated in every corner. There were even some in the bathroom. Screws were always turning up in unexpected places.

In hopes of growing his clientele, Lulu put up a sign in the building entryway saying that he could repair any kind of machine — electrical, electronic, or mechanical — for a flat rate of thirty euros. In the following days, everyone in the entire building came to pay us a visit. I found the incongruous possessions of our neighbors rather amusing. Thérèse on the third floor brought him a vibrator. She begged us not to say anything to her husband. For her pleasure, Lulu increased its power. Because of his great resourcefulness, some neighbors gave him a bit more money or brought us a lasagna. And even though it was difficult with the little money he collected, Lulu made a point of paying half the rent.

And so, in the space of a few weeks, I became financially independent. My father was flabbergasted. He was pleased with the turn my life was taking. He never stopped asking, 'When am I going to meet him, this boyfriend of yours? When are you bringing him over?' I promised that it would be soon. He asked if I was sure I didn't need any money, if I was absolutely certain that my bank account wasn't in the red. He needed reassurance that what I was telling him was true: he had seen plenty of TV shows about young people who fall into sex work. I was unfazed, I told him, 'Don't worry, don't worry, I'm only out on the streets when I'm taking a walk.' My father always ended our calls by saying that he'd seen me on TV. I knew this wasn't true, but I laughed anyway. I think he drew a certain pride from it. All the neighbors, friends of the family, and distant relatives had written to me after I was hired. Not only to congratulate me for landing a job, but for landing this one in particular. I don't know what they were imagining, but it seemed to really impress them. 'Our little girl works in television. For a big channel too, not France 5 or Téva.' And my father would follow up with, 'She got into the field thanks to me. All those hours on the couch watching TV, turns out it was useful! I always knew she'd succeed.' I never contradicted their fantasies; I liked feeding their imaginations.

The reality was less glamorous. Yes, they had hired me, but everyone at the studio looked right through me. I was the invisible woman. Although my first name was easy to remember, everyone got it wrong. So I answered to Leïla, Laura, Sonia, Sophia, Emma. It didn't matter, really. On the other hand, I was starting to get closer with Sandrine. I wouldn't go so far as to say we'd become friends, but I was, at least, learning to tolerate her daily hysteria and her contempt for ugly people. After all, that attitude had been imposed upon her. She didn't decide anything. I had managed to butter her up with triple-chocolate cookies from the vending machine. Little by little, she started confiding in me. In return, I offered up a compliment on her handbag. 'It's from Vinted, actually. I would never have been able to afford it new. My boyfriend thinks I'm an idiot, that I spend a stupid amount on that site. It leaves him with less money for betting on sports. He doesn't get it. You take two steps on the street and BAM!, a Chanel ad, two more steps and POW!, a Louis Vuitton. I want to be like them. When I was younger, I was almost a model, you know. But I wasn't tall enough.' I asked her how she'd ended up working for the show. A degree in communications, some event planning, and a chance encounter with Bertrand, whom she admired and who had found her this job. 'He even told me that he'd invite me to his vacation home in St. Barts one day. It's made entirely of marble. Well, so far, still no invite, but ... we're better off here than in prison, right?' I didn't know whether to laugh or be horrified by Sandrine's question. At least she was down to earth. A welcome perspective.

As soon as I entered the apartment, the birds gave me an enthusiastic welcome, screeching and cheeping joyously. I spent a long time examining their feathers. Red. Orange. Green. I liked how they pecked at their seeds. When I held them in my hand, it tickled. I pet their heads, each in their turn, so as not to incite jealousy. They nestled together and groomed one another. It was as if I were seeing us, Lulu and me, in a mirror.

4

That day, when I pushed open the door, the hangar was submerged in a troubling silence. Second-guessing myself, I glanced quickly at my phone calendar: it wasn't a holiday. Sidling up to me, Sandrine explained: Bertrand has a cold, he can't film today. I was about to turn around and go back home. I was already thinking about the softness of our mattress and Lulu's expression, so happy to see that I'd returned. Marc dashed my dreams.

'We're going to use the time for a *team building* session.'

'Are we going to Parc Astérix?'

'No, Sandrine, we don't have the budget for that, as you know ...'

She seemed disappointed. Noticing my confusion at the English expression, she turned to me.

'*Team building* means bonding with your colleagues. You'll see, it's great. It's very important for solidarity.'

'Hang on, they already make us spend eight hours a day together, they can't force us to like each other, too.'

A make-up artist who seemed to notice me for the first time tapped me on the shoulder.

'Haha, good one, doll! Everyone adores each other here, you know that.'

So we formed a large circle and sat on the ground, like an Alcoholics Anonymous meeting, or a cult. Marc presided over the ceremony.

'Each person will say something about another person's good qualities. Rapid fire, without thinking too much about it. It has to come from the heart.'

Adjectives zoomed past in every direction. It was an eruption, a volcano of compliments. When my turn came, I was unprepared. Everyone was staring at me.

'Sandrine has eyes.'

'What about them?' Marc growled.

'They're blue.'

'Come on, are you a moron? Having eyes isn't a good quality.'

'Actually, technically speaking, the word "quality" comprises the characteristics belonging to an individual, whether innate or …'

'Blah blah blah, "technically speaking", blah blah blah, you're talking gibberish, sweetheart. A compliment, is that so difficult? Okay, next person.'

After everyone had a turn, we tightened the circle for a

group hug. It smelled like sweat and hypocrisy. Obviously, no one had managed to sum up my good qualities. I was pretty bummed about screwing up the exercise. I was tired of being scorned. The new girl people subtly mock. I wanted to be liked, to belong in this group, even if it was just a conglomerate of solitary people united solely by the goal of earning enough money to feed and house themselves.

'Don't worry about it,' Sandrine comforted me, 'next time we'll go to Parc Astérix, it'll be better.'

I wanted to wrap my arms around her.

When I got home that night, Lulu was on the couch. He was jumping around like a flea, biting his nails, pulling his hair. In his left hand was a glue gun. In his right hand, a ticket. He was riveted to the TV screen. I could see the show reflected in his eyes: the lottery.

'Don't tell me you play! People never win, it's a scam. You know you have a better chance of being struck by lightning than drawing the winning numbers?'

'Shush, killjoy. Lightning struck when I met you, so why not? I have the first two numbers.'

But the following numbers weren't a match. Furious, Lulu did something completely unexpected. He crumpled the paper in his hand to a tiny ball and swallowed it. I laughed so hard I almost choked. We ate frozen pizzas and watched a movie, and then we had sex. With Lulu, at least, I felt like I was important, and the rest didn't matter. Thanks to him, our minimum-wage life wasn't so bad, was maybe even kind of nice, in the end.

The next morning as I entered the kitchen to make my tea, I found Lulu hunched over his soft-boiled egg, lost in thought. His hand was lazily dipping a piece of bread into the yolk. The little comma on his cheek had disappeared. 'Everything okay?' I asked, but he must not have heard me. He kissed me on the forehead and continued eating in silence. I ventured the question again. Lulu finally lifted his eyes from his plate.

'I have a lump in my throat.'

'Yeah, Lulu, it's called an Adam's apple. You're only noticing it now?'

He didn't lift his head. Bad sign. I sought another explanation. Maybe Lulu had the same lump that had been haunting me since I was a teenager? It was probably contagious. I was angry at myself. He seemed so worried.

'My love, I get it, you know. You don't feel valued by our society? You feel lackluster, like you're a nobody to the people around you? Remember what Nietzsche said, Lulu: "Become who you are."'

'Anna, what are you on about?'

Uh oh — not the same lump. Out of ideas, I thought of

our birds. For a few days, one of them had been in a gloomy mood.

'Is it because of Estragon? You shouldn't worry about him. Maybe he's just sad.'

'No, Anna, you're not getting it, I have a lump in my throat, literally. Feel it. I made an appointment with a doctor this morning.'

There was a growth on the left side. I felt stupid, unable to find the words to comfort him. From the door, I simply promised that everything would be okay. I didn't turn around as I walked down the sidewalk. There was no need, I knew he was watching me.

The day whizzed by. Same choreography. Arms up. Laughter. Clap clap for applause. To enhance the volunteer audience, production had brought in professional spectators. Their job was even crazier than mine. These people were paid to watch shows of all kinds. I had no idea what degree people earned to enter this trade, but their expertise was obvious. The professional laughers never grew tired. Their vocal cords vibrated on command, loud and clear. Some had a unique laugh. I loved listening to them. It made me think of the soloists at a philharmonic concert.

'What did the doctor say?'

'Not much, nothing abnormal. A bad sore throat.'

That night, Lulu and I were spooning, my back warmed

by his stomach and vice versa. He couldn't fall asleep at first, so I offered to make him tea to help his sore throat. He squeezed my arm hard and told me he loved me.

Around two in the morning, my phone vibrated. I tried to ignore it, but it kept ringing. I picked up and heard Sophie's panicked voice:

'Why does God exist?'

'You couldn't think of a bigger question for the middle of the night?'

'According to Descartes, sorry, I'm deep in *Meditations*. The first proof, I think I understand, but not the second, the ontological argument.'

'It's actually more of an ontological-axiological argument, because he starts from the presupposition that existence has greater value than nonexistence. Grosso modo, it's better to be than not to be, and since God is perfect, he must be, by definition.'

'Aaaaah, okay. And all that for him to be killed by Nietzsche after?'

'Yeah, tough luck, huh … And according to Deleuze, he's a lobster with two claws, talk about a fall from grace …'

'What? Really?'

'Listen, you're better off not talking at all about God in your essay, okay?'

All this in a murmur so as not to wake Lulu. Satisfied, she let me go, and I was able to fall back asleep. But it didn't last long: around 6 am, I felt something moving at my side. Thinking it was Sophie again, I was ready to curse her when I saw that it wasn't my phone vibrating, but Lulu. He was having intense spasms. Contorting in every direction. Terrible pain in his stomach. He was hawking up phlegm. Something wanted to come out, he said. I asked him if he needed medicine, but Lulu rushed to the bathroom.

'Maybe it was the leftover pizza, we shouldn't have eaten it,' I called to him through the door.

His only response was a faint gurgling. I listened for the sound of the flush indicating that everything was okay, but he called to me:

'Anna, come look, there's something strange in the toilet bowl.'

'Lulu, I adore you, but not enough to inspect your vomit.'

'Come here, seriously, it's really bizarre.'

They were expecting me at the studio, I was tired and irritated. I extricated myself from the bed, grumbling my desire to get back in. I peeked through the doorway. Zenithal angle of his head and the pool of murky water. An object was floating at the back of the toilet bowl. Lulu plunged his hand inside to grab it.

'That's disgusting, what are you doing? You're going to make me puke, too.'

He wasn't listening. I thought to myself, *that's it, he's totally lost it, I'll have to have him committed.* All I wanted was a lover, a simple passion, not psychiatric hospitals with padded walls. Meanwhile, Lulu pulled from the toilet bowl something that looked like paper and unfolded it. Our jaws dropped.

'Are you seeing what I'm seeing?'

'You're completely insane, you swallowed money?'

'No, I swear I didn't. Or if I did, I don't remember ... Maybe it happened by accident?'

'You think you swallowed twenty bucks without knowing it? Have you ever vomited ... that before?'

'Yes, of course, Anna, every morning. Haven't you noticed my private jet parked outside the building?'

'No need to be sarcastic, I'm just trying to understand ... Does it hurt anywhere in particular? Is your stomach gurgling?'

'No, not exactly. Go on, you're going to be late. No need for the great Bertrand to notice you're missing. I'll be fine, it must have been an accident.'

'Are you sure? While I'm gone ... I don't know, don't eat anything and drink some water?'

'Ha, that's your best advice? Go, really, I'm going to lie down.'

'Call me if things get any worse? Call me, okay?'

On my way to work, I thought of nothing but that bill. How did it end up inside Lulu? I opened my wallet to see if any money was missing. Bingo: it was empty! A second later, I remembered that I never had cash. Maybe it was a gimmick from a joke shop, like a pack of chewing gum that gives an electric shock to whoever touches it, or a fake latex scar. But deep down, I knew that this was different. He had seemed really sick. Maybe the bill had been stuck under the pizza, and he hadn't noticed it while he was eating? But the probability that a bill would wind up there was slim. I performed my usual gestures on set while my mind was elsewhere.

Under the circumstances, I hadn't had time to buy myself something to eat. Before or after work, I usually assembled my 'lunch box'. Quick trip to the supermarket, either very early in the morning, or very late at night. At those odd hours, I was surrounded by an eclectic mix of people. Overwhelmed mothers pushing carts crammed with kids and food. They bought in bulk. Canned food. Powdered milk. Cereal bars. Cordon bleus. All in packs of four, five, even six. The children whined when the green beans landed in the trolley. They screamed when their mothers skipped the candy aisles. There were also a few businessmen, more well-off people. Superior loners. They bought individual trays to heat up in the microwave. Quick and easy. Remove the packaging. Pierce the seal. One to three minutes, and you're good to go.

I wandered through the aisles hunched over. Animalian gait. I bought the least expensive products, at the very bottom of the shelves. Invisible to the businessmen. Under their radar. I had to check the expiration dates — supermarkets couldn't care less about palming off expired products on the poor. Only off-brand. Packaging that makes you want to shoot yourself in the head. No need for flourishes, their customers only need to feed themselves. Fill them with saturated fat, carcinogenic ingredients. All natural? Dream on. A mix of dyes and preservatives, some artificial flavoring, and call it a day. A week's worth of groceries for sixty-seven euros. Shoot, that's two euros more than I have. So much for the shower gel — I'll put some water in the old bottle. It won't lather much, but it'll still do the job.

There was nowhere to grab a bite near the studio. So, at break time, the group split into two categories. The first, of which I was a part, were the gofers with their plastic Tupperware and their hey-can-you-spare-some-salt-please-I-forgot-to-season-mine. Men and women in black, sometimes even the contestants. In a dressing room with comfy couches, the second category: Bertrand, the producers, when they wanted to check up on things, and the members of the jury, starlets from the 2000s and popular singers. A van came specially to provide them with provisions. High-quality catered dishes from well-known establishments. The first name of each person was handwritten on the brown paper bags. The aroma emanated to us; Sandrine inhaled deeply. The chefs knew their allergies by heart. Their preferences had been taken into consideration; constant attention was given to the chosen ones. Meanwhile, for us, it was a different world. If the second lighting engineer accidentally swallowed peanut oil and his throat swelled to the point of edema, hardly anyone would notice.

The divide was immutable. Through the partition, we could hear the sound of their forks and their gentle laughter. Carefree. So different from the laughter of the crowd. Silk to the ear. I would have loved to have the same laugh, for the chef of a restaurant to know that I wasn't allergic to anything, but that I didn't like peas. For lack of a better alternative, I settled for cookies from the vending machine, bought with the red and yellow coins fished out of the bottom of my pocket.

Lulu was ashen, even paler than usual, nearly transparent. Drool had dried at the corner of his lips. Half-human, half-ectoplasm. An empty membrane. I avoided touching him for fear he might liquify from my embrace. His eyes had changed color, now almost turquoise. I didn't ask how he was feeling, as it was obvious that things had taken a turn for the worse. He stared at me and recoiled cautiously. In front of him, a basin filled with blue paper: twenty-euro bills. There were at least fifty.

'It's been nonstop all day.'

'This is really bad. We should go to the emergency room.'

'And what would we tell them, that I'm puking up cash? That I've transformed into an ATM?'

He spat out his phrases in a hoarse voice.

'Lulu, we can't mess around with your health. If this is what's coming out, can you imagine what must be happening on the inside?'

'Drop it, Anna. It'll stop, I'm sure it will. What if they take me away? Do tests on me like a lab rat?'

'You're right, we should keep it a secret, at least for a few days. My poor love, your throat must hurt, paper can cut.'

After a moment, Lulu looked at me timidly.

'Do you think these are real?' he finally said.

'There's only one way to find out. Stay there, I'll handle it.'

First, I drew the curtains and prepared warm milk with honey to ease his pain. Then I opened the bathroom cabinet and plugged in the hairdryer. The bills were slimy and crumpled. I grabbed one, flattened it with the palm of my hand and held it under the warm air, turning it over several times. The result remained disgusting. Dried bile covered the paper with an off-white crust that I had to scratch off with my nail. After some effort, the bill finally resumed its proper form.

Outside, it was already night and the cold stung severely. I amused myself by pretending to smoke when I exhaled, and then I turned my mind back to my urgent mission. The tabac I was looking for was at the end of the street. A bar-tabac, in fact. A betting shop with cigarettes, scratch-off tickets, Picon beer, and peanuts sprinkled with thirty-six different samples of urine. It was run by Christelle, who wasn't a person to be messed with. Things could kick off quickly, or so she threatened the notorious drunkards. You could only pay by cash, and with each purchase, she would closely inspect the bills. With an expert eye, Christelle felt them, spread them, scrutinized them against the light. And when people teased her, she always replied: 'I'm actually a DGSE agent, this is just my cover.' Nothing escaped her.

I approached timidly and handed her the blue bill.

'Well, thanks, sweetheart, but what do you want?'

'Oh, uh, a pack of gum and a can of Coke, please.'

She carried out the usual inspection maneuvers and then opened the cash register. Jackpot. Foolproof test. She handed me the change and I took off running, as if I were afraid that she would grab me or report me to the Bank of France. I climbed the stairs two at a time and told Lulu everything. He couldn't believe it. This is impossible, what's going on? He didn't have much time to puzzle over it before a new wave of bills was already pouring out of his mouth. I held his head back for a good part of the night.

5

The goal of the weekend was to figure out a plan. We dried all the bills, and I counted them tirelessly. Two thousand five hundred and twenty euros. Lulu was exhausted. In a few days, he had lost weight, and his body was ravaged by nervous tics. Sometimes, the bills got stuck in his windpipe, like hairballs in cats. He would clear his throat, coughing, and finally pull out the phlegmy heap by hand. The insides of his cheeks, covered in tiny cuts, bled constantly. Lulu applied a layer of cream for canker sores that didn't help at all. On the contrary, the wounds were becoming infected. Sometimes, he would spit out pus.

'If you don't want to see a doctor, you could at least go to a dentist.'

'It will heal, and I promise, it's not that bad. The most painful part is that you don't want to kiss me anymore.'

What an idiot. I drew near his splitting lips and planted

mine onto them. He was trying to reassure me because he loved me. But, faced with his suffering body, I panicked. I was afraid of losing him, and I had no idea how to help.

That Saturday, we bought a nice breakfast at the boulangerie to restore his strength: several pain au chocolats and even a freshly squeezed orange juice. On second thought, I realized that this would probably sting his mouth terribly. However, Lulu remained imperturbable; he didn't want to ruin the moment. And that wasn't all: rather than going back to the apartment, he told me that he had a surprise for me.

We took the metro to the Champs-Élysées. Normally, we never set foot there. Really, there was nothing for us there. The large avenue unfurled before us. Lots of cars with powerful engines. Hordes of tourists with their arms full of bags. Beggars calling out to people who never stopped. Trees flaunting their bare branches, dressed only in newly strung Christmas garlands. After a few minutes of walking, Lulu stopped in front of a luxury boutique.

'Go on, Anna, go in. Pick out something you like, it's on me.'

'It's too expensive, Lulu, you're crazy. We don't have the money …'

'The money? My pockets are stuffed with bills. Go on, please, you work so hard, it would make me happy.'

As soon as I walked in the store, I could hear the snickering of the other customers. Laughs as crystalline as those that reverberated on the other side of the TV studio's dividing wall. I let myself be soothed by the clothes, with their refined textures, and the intoxicating fragrance of the diffuser. We stuck out like sore thumbs, Lulu and I, so the security guard was following us around. My eyes landed on a purse. Thick leather. Brand name big enough to be noticeable, small enough not to be vulgar. I turned to look at Lulu, my eyes wide with hope, and he acquiesced. A second later, I changed my mind and set the purse back down.

'No, no, we have to be sensible, and anyway, it's not very me, that purse. I don't care about this stuff — let's go back home and get under the covers.'

'Out of the question. Take it and stop feeling guilty.'

We walked to the register. The saleswoman seemed shocked. She repeated the price several times to be sure that we understood what store we were in. Cash, please. She was even more shocked. As soon as the purchase was made, I pressed the purse to my chest for fear it might be stolen. On the way home, Lulu gagged a few times, and we hurried back. Once the apartment door was closed behind us, he could empty his guts in peace.

It was time to get serious. On Monday, Lulu would go to the bank to deposit the cash into our accounts. In order to get a clearer idea for the future. Be responsible. Save up for an apartment. Life insurance. Household accounting and an Excel spreadsheet. Meanwhile, the bills were drying on lines that I had stretched across the living room. The heater in the bathroom was covered in bills, too. A giant aquarium: blue everywhere you looked. The air had become unbreathable. I had to wear a snorkel mask, for the odor. I sprayed air freshener everywhere. Vanilla and cotton flower. The last thing we needed was for our neighbors to think we were hiding a dead body.

'Tomorrow, take a walk around the building, okay? So that Thérèse and the others don't think I murdered you.'

I spent the day on Sunday making little bundles of two hundred euros that I stashed around the bedroom as well as I could. We lived in a neighborhood that tarnished the image of the City of Lights. One that the mayor would have liked to unload on another commune. One that was the subject of immersive reportage following police officers, broadcast late night on the TNT channels and designed to make you paranoid, make you think a man dressed in black is waiting for you at every street corner to stick a knife in your throat, fleece you, or steal your iPhone. To my great surprise, I had succumbed to this psychosis. It was so rare that I owned something precious. I had to protect it.

Sunday night, as a reward for all our organization and effort, we went to have dinner at a restaurant. For the first time, we double locked our door. I noticed that there were no prices listed on the menu: an old-school custom. For the occasion, I'd put on a slinky dress, a bit of fabric that I thought was very elegant. However, observing the women at the tables around us, I could see I had missed the mark entirely, dressed like the housekeeper in their countryside villa. Lulu was completely oblivious and smiling like an idiot. 'You're stunning, Anna.' He'd made the effort to put on a tie he'd worn only once before, at his baccalaureate ceremony. It was too short, but so long as it was tucked into his jacket, that went unnoticed. He scratched his ankles often because he had stashed some bills in his socks, in case we were mugged on the way.

I tried to guess the price of each dish. Was lobster more expensive than foie gras? Or was it the other way around? There were some dishes whose names went on and on, each ingredient served on a bed made of another ingredient. Strange vegetables, not the ones at the supermarket. Same for the fish. Nothing breaded, only mouthwatering varieties like flounder and cuttlefish. Even the bread promised to be crustier. I ordered blindly, trying to avoid at all costs showing that we understood nothing of the menu. Lulu chose the wine, pretending to know the grape varietals. Exorbitantly priced glasses of red. There were too many pieces of silverware. Three knives, two forks, two glasses. It was too much. Faced with so much opulence, intimidated by the setting, we stayed completely silent. Lulu pulled on his tie to loosen the knot, the anxiety of another expulsion lurking at the bottom of his stomach. The bathroom door in our line of vision, just in case. To pass the time, we listened to the conversations of the neighboring tables. They talked about the CAC 40 and ISF. It all went over our heads.

'Anna, do you think we'll return soon to our chalet in Serre Chevalier?'

'Oh yes, darling, the ambiance is idyllic, a true little paradise. It's too bad the resort is getting more and more popular, don't you think?'

'Ah, don't get me started! All that riffraff crammed into those charmless buildings ...'

Relaxed again, we snorted into the immaculate, thick linen napkins. Our laughter became convulsive. The flames of the candles decorating our tables flickered. We were hamming it up, exaggerated bourgeois accents to boot. The purple wall hangings transformed before our eyes into theater curtains. The parquet floor became our stage.

'Excuse me, monsieur, I must ask you to quiet down. Some of the guests have complained that you are laughing too loudly.'

Soon the color of my face matched the curtains. But Lulu, he continued the comedy act. His greatest role.

'You are right to excuse yourself. I'm laughing too loudly? I've never been treated like this in my life. It's scandalous. We're leaving, immediately. The check, please.'

He winked at me.

'I've always dreamed of making a scene.'

'Yes, but it's always the same people who suffer the consequences,' I said, sobering up, watching the waiter, terribly contrite, rush to the register.

SELF-WORTH

When he placed the check on the table, Lulu apologized. He took the bills from his socks and handed them to him.

'You're twenty euros short, monsieur,' the waiter said, visibly disgusted.

'Oh yes, just a moment, please.'

Lulu headed for the bathroom. Meanwhile, I tried to avoid the eyes of the crowd that was staring at us avidly, in anticipation of another spectacle. So distinguished in their overpriced suits. So silent. So polite. So well mannered. So dull.

Lulu came back a few minutes later. The bill was still full of saliva, so he wiped it on his pants. We left with dignity, arm in arm, and, by way of goodbye, pressed ourselves against the glass to pull faces at the diners.

I fell asleep quickly, my stomach full of delicious dishes I'd tasted for the first time. Since the beginning of my studies, I had become accustomed to simple meals, primarily composed of potato chips. In the middle of the night, I heard Schubert: Lulu had fallen behind on his week's work, so between trips to the bathroom, he repaired our neighbors' appliances. I'd hidden in my coat a few pieces of premium bread for Vladimir and Estragon. They had a right to celebrate, too. Their chirping intensified and complemented the orchestra. Estragon seemed to be back in good spirits.

6

Every Wednesday, as promised, I went to help Sophie with her revision. The first time, stepping back in her studio again, I thought she'd been robbed. The apartment was in an unbelievable state. Open books were strewn across the floor, a stench of mildew emanated from clothes left in the washing machine for days or even weeks and, above all, dozens and dozens of packets of instant noodles covered every surface.

'Are you preparing for a siege?'

'Leave me alone, I don't have much time to cook. Quiz me on Aristotelian physics.'

Sophie was scribbling on flashcards that she placed methodically in little binders. They were the only organized thing in her bedroom.

'Especially the things that I highlighted in yellow, those are the most important.'

Absolutely everything was highlighted in yellow. Except the connecting words such as 'by' or 'thus'. I spoke the first word, and, like a trained monkey, Sophie took it from there. Her eyes looked to the right when she was searching for the words. The exercise proved painstaking because as soon as she made a mistake, she would slam the desk with her fist (or her head), repeating that she would never pass, that it was too difficult, that she was an idiot. I wished I could tell her to stop — seeing her in that state upset me and summoned bad memories. It wasn't just studying anymore; it was a marathon.

At the same time, on my end, I had done everything I'd been told to do. Work hard and you'll be rewarded. Get a head start. On what? My thesis, typed up, bound, the score marked in thick red pen: 18. An excellent job, my advisor had testified. The day of the defense, my elbows ached from all those hours spent at the library flipping through books. The large university gates were open, as if solely for me. My head was spinning with plans. The professor's beaming face welcomed me. A very thorough work of research, few things to find fault with, yes, decidedly, you are a good philosopher, an apprentice philosopher but a philosopher all the same. Up to your ears in potential. My cheeks were red with embarrassment and satisfaction. So I charged, like a goat, head first, ready to smash it all down.

I got carried away, I brought up my dissertation proposal, 'Transhumanism between performance and erasure', the desire to continue the project, the possibility of extending the research. He chuckled with embarrassment, lowered his eyes.

'Do you have the means to finance your dissertation?'

'What do you mean? I was thinking of getting a scholarship, a doctoral contract.'

'Anna, the number of doctoral contracts given out can be counted on one hand. And there are too many of you — some contracts are filled two years in advance. You won't be able to get one. If I were you, I would look for a real job. Humanities academia is a little like the *Titanic*: the orchestra continues to play, but the building is crumbling all around it. Just look at the cracks in the ceiling.'

I thought it was a metaphor, but no, he was actually pointing at the ceiling. A brown water stain had outlined a large ring.

'What about teaching? If I earn my teaching degree, I could do research after? Or write a book, host symposia?'

He didn't respond. I took his silence for a polite 'no'. Just like that, the social mobility elevator had brought me back to the basement. Last stop, everybody off. The goat horns retracted, my chin started to tremble, but I managed to swallow my pride despite the lump. Stiff upper lip. A proper handshake, *au revoir monsieur, yes, I'll keep you updated.* Do you have a plan B? *More like a plan E for employment office, like the rest of my classmates.* Haha, you have a sense of humor at least. *Thank you, thank you, no future but at least there's that.* When I left, I was already dreading having to call my father.

'So, at least 16, I bet?'

'18, actually, Papa.'

'Bravo, my girl! You must be so happy! So, what's next? The thesis fellowship is all set?'

'Not exactly ...'

'Oh, but ... what will you do now, my darling? I told you, philosophy isn't really a profession. Maybe you should have studied accounting, like me. Well, at least you had some fun. Come to the house tonight, I'll make crepes, we still have to celebrate your degree!'

So, for my father, dissecting Heidegger's *Being and Time* through text commentary for six hours straight was a barrel of laughs. The truth is that he wasn't wrong: my degree *was* superfluous because it had led to nothing. I pretended to be brimming with goals for the future, I had a drink with some friends, and I still felt the lump in my throat when I went to bed that night. Thesis filed. Hidden away. Left behind. It was time to move on.

Normally, the final moments of our cramming sessions were dedicated to comforting Sophie. I would cradle her in my arms, trying to find encouraging words. I could have plunged back into Epicurean philosophy, but it was too much work, so I tried to appease her with quotations taken from the Internet. 'Happiness is not always in an eternally blue sky, but in the simplest aspects of life' by Confucius, or else the Indian proverb 'If you see everything in gray, move the elephant!' Sophie sniffled and opened a pack of instant noodles.

'You're not going to cook them?'

'I told you I don't have time to cook.'

She chomped into the block, nonchalant, after sprinkling it with salt and pepper.

'You're sure you don't want to try? It's not so bad.'

Metro. Metro. RER. Then something incredible happened. When I opened the large metallic door, I was immediately welcomed by a 'Bonjour, Anna' from Marc: he had remembered my name. The others, too. Smiles galore, and people moved out of my way as I passed. Would you like a coffee? Despite my utter confusion, I felt like I was floating on a cloud.

'Your purse is amazing, it looks new! Don't tell me it's new!'

Sandrine threw herself at me. She had a bruise under one eye and had tried to hide it with a lock of hair. You could see the thick layer of concealer that was meant to camouflage the injury, but the tint was too green and only accentuated it.

'Yes, it is, it was a gift from my boyfriend. But what happened to you? Is everything okay?'

'Oh, that, don't worry about it. I ran into a door.'

She shrugged her shoulders to emphasize her absent-mindedness. Then she changed the subject:

'Wow, is your guy a stockbroker or something? Does he have a friend for me?'

Excited, she turned the purse every which way, even shoved her head inside.

'Is this the new season's model? I saw the ad on an Abribus. You're so lucky. Did you change something about your hair, too? No? You should. Maybe straighten it to make it shinier?'

Bertrand gathered us together in the large hall. The situation was critical. One of the rare times I had seen him without makeup. I hardly recognized him. An old man, his forehead like wrinkled parchment paper, his pot belly poorly concealed beneath his shirt. The show ratings were catastrophic. Bertrand was crying foul. They were trying to oust him, he was sure of it. He gesticulated in every direction, punctuated his speech with 'Don't you see?' and, under duress, his followers, which now included me, nodded their heads reverently. It was a conspiracy, the numbers were categorical. The spectators were sick of songs. That's why production had decided to pull a 180. They were launching a new series. You have to be always reinventing yourself, always surprising people. New decor, new jury, new concept. The weather was gloomy, the days at the office exhausting. What do people want? To laugh. That was what the producers were pushing. The show would now be a string of comedians performing stand-up routines for a few minutes each. The network was demanding joy, but also violence. Some artists would have to be booed at. It was the Roman games.

For Sandrine, this changed nothing. Whether it was a TV shopping channel, political commentary, or a cooking show, her work didn't differ a bit: the ugly ones still sat in the back. My objective, however, would be different. The laughs not only had to be audible but would constitute the very identity of the show. A hurricane. A torrential downpour. A tropical monsoon. The production manager made extensive use of metaphor. I would have a lot on my plate.

Before the recording began, Bertrand asked me to join him in his office. Well, not exactly — he snapped his fingers in my general direction, and I deduced that I was meant to follow him. He worked in a warm room full of leather club chairs. I couldn't stop myself from discreetly caressing one. On the walls: his TV awards. A myriad of photos of him in enviable situations. Bertrand shaking hands with Iggy Pop. Bertrand having a drink with Alicia Keys. Bertrand in a heated discussion with the President of the Republic. That one was printed poster size to commemorate the importance of the event.

'Right, since it's your first day, I wanted to introduce myself in person. You must have heard a lot about me? My reputation often precedes me, as they say.'

It had been more than six months since I started working on the premises. But I didn't dare contradict him. He told me his entire trajectory. Difficult childhood in a working-class neighborhood. Son of immigrants. Rough assimilation and bullying at school. Meeting his mentor. Work. Sweat. Discipline. And vindication. His first time on television, back when there was only one network. I listened to him piously. I would have almost felt sorry for him if my colleagues hadn't warned me that it was all bullshit. I wasn't angry; one must carefully craft their lore. Fashion the myth. In this milieu, fabricating a story for oneself was par for the course. I grinned and bore it until he was finished listing the contract offers raining down miraculously on his head.

'I have a vacation home in St. Barts. We could go there together one of these days, it's made entirely of marble.'

Another snap of the fingers and a glance towards the door: I was dismissed. Just before I walked out, Bertrand said to me:

'Very nice purse, Anna. It's the dress and shoes that'll have to change now. To match, you see.'

I couldn't believe my ears. The contours of my existence were finally taking shape in the eyes of others, as if through some kind of enchantment. I was materializing.

The first series in the new format was a wild success.

SELF-WORTH

The French called for more, they love a good laugh. Just after work and before the seriousness of the news. Blessed hour. The ratings soared. At the end of the recording, I felt twice as tired as I had after the music series, and my salary hadn't doubled to match.

Meanwhile, Lulu had gone to the bank. He had replenished his account, and mine too. It was enough money to cover two months of rent, the electricity and gas bills, and even our Navigo passes. A new batch of cash was drying on the line. He had gone back to work with renewed fervor. Bruno on the fourth floor had brought him a microwave that was proving complicated to repair. Between the bills and the broken objects, we were starting to be seriously tight on space. It took me several minutes to find Vladimir and Estragon's cage.

'Do you think we should move?'

'Yeah, why not, you want to rent something bigger?'

'Rent? No, Lulu, with all the money you're coughing up, we could buy. That way, it would be ours forever. Real estate is the safest bet there is.'

7

The back room of the bank smelled like patchouli and disinfectant. It made me sneeze. Leïla, our advisor, spoke with a honeyed voice and the softness of a lullaby. She welcomed us with a smile that took up her entire face. 'What can I do for you? A loan, yes of course, it's a good time, interest rates are extremely low, you should definitely invest, can I offer you coffee? Tea? Buying property together requires a relationship built on trust, so let's get to know each other. I work for the wellbeing of my clients, a sort of doctor if you like, a money doctor, hehehe. You are a bit young, it's true. But young people are full of vim and vigor. And those who study business start to earn good money very early, a better living even than some of the older executives. Have you brought your documents? I'll have to take a look at them to offer you the best proposal.'

As soon as Leïla opened the plastic folder, her smile

disappeared altogether. Her brow furrowed. I felt like I was back at the employment office. As if she thought we were pulling a prank on her. She started sweating, pulled at her collar, ran her hand through her hair nervously.

'With a minimum wage job and you, monsieur, uh, you've described yourself as a "handyman", is that right? The bank will never give you a loan. You don't even have enough for a down payment.'

'Oh yes we do!'

That's when Lulu whipped out the black canvas sports bag. He pulled on the zipper, pleased to prove to Leïla that we had the means.

Leïla's eyes bulged, three millimeters away from falling out of their socket. Frozen between attraction and horror.

'But how is it possible that you have so much cash?'

In her words, we heard the accusation of 'drug traffickers', 'prostitution', and an array of other illegal activities. Two bandits in an episode of *Enquête exclusive*. We stammered. Could we tell her the truth? Lulu was turning words around in his mouth. She would never believe our story. In the end he claimed to have sold some valuable objects. Leïla kept the same expression, without blinking, recoiling in her chair as if Lulu were about to brandish a weapon. She adopted a tone that signified, 'Don't take me for an idiot, but this time I'll let it slide.' It couldn't happen again, otherwise she would be forced to report it as suspicious to the police.

Rejects of the adult night club.

I could tell that Lulu's stomach was in knots, and not from his illness.

'Forget it, I wasn't feeling her anyway. We'll find another solution, my Lulu, I promise.'

My colleague Thierry knew his way around shady dealings. Troubled past as a bodyguard for a celebrity, a high-speed drug smuggler, and a total junkie. Now he's fallen in line, in his words, content with his bird perch, his camera, and his uniform of T-shirt and black jeans. But every so often he still turned up with knick-knacks that had fallen off a truck, which he resold for next to nothing. Counterfeit iPhones, silk scarves, lipsticks from a new coveted collection. Sandrine was always pestering him: 'Is there Dior this time?' I felt like he could help us.

During lunch break, after responding to a panicked text from Sophie informing her that yes, Husserlian phenomenology was essential for understanding Sartrian existentialism, I walked over to Thierry. I climbed the rungs. They sagged beneath my weight, even though I wasn't big. The ladder was swaying in every direction. From above, the others seemed minuscule. An anthill. Everyone bustled around the queen, Marc the floor manager, who was speaking into his headset and giving orders to everyone, because the break wasn't really a break. Being up so high was pretty cool. A parenthesis of calm. Little bubble of peace above the frenzy. I even spotted Bertrand's bald head when he emerged from his ivory tower to take an important phone call. Thierry showed me how it all worked. He tested his camera by roaming through the studio. A few close-up shots of other workers. He scrutinized the disputes of illegitimate couples and the whisperings of disgruntled employees. He had me look through the viewfinder and pressed on buttons to zoom in or change the angle. The world is incredible when we can choose its frame.

Thierry was smoking a cigarillo. Smoking wasn't allowed, but he didn't care. I appreciated his attitude. I had thought about it all morning and deemed that the best solution was to be as direct as possible, while remaining mysterious about the provenance of our dough.

'Your boyfriend churns out a lot of money, I see. What's his line of work? Weed, coke, smack?

'No, no, it's a little more complicated than that.'

'You're right, it's none of my business.'

A discreet man, a gentleman, this Thierry. I told him about our misadventure at the bank and the impossibility of taking out a loan. I tried to guess the expression on his face through the thick cloud of smoke he was spewing, spreading an acrid odor of damp cardboard. He told me that he would take care of the apartment. He knew a guy for cash renters, but we couldn't be owners right away. We'd have to be patient for a while, until he could find a way to launder our money. Meanwhile, the most important thing was to get rid of it, and not to keep any cash at our place in case the bank advisor changed her mind and reported us. He was a pro. I left reassured.

The floor was covered in blue bills. Lulu was vomiting almost continuously, so much that he didn't have time to hang them up. A deluge. He looked more and more like the heroin addicts who hung around our building. Despite his efforts to seem calm, his worry was palpable. Sometimes I could hear him sobbing in the bathroom. Trying to be subtle, he felt, groped, inspected himself nonstop, the way you might prod a piece of meat that's been in the fridge a little too long, to check whether it's spoiled. But when I was around, Lulu was always smiling. I explained Thierry's plan to him. He was dubious: how would we get rid of all this money? I wanted to go out shopping, but he had too much work. He was interrupted every three minutes, and the broken objects were piling up. His agile hands couldn't get into a rhythm anymore. But he didn't want to stop working. He gripped his scrap metal with all his strength, the welder working at full capacity. 'If I stop, I'll be useless,' he repeated. To give him some relief, I took charge. I left with my pockets overflowing and my purse full of bills.

My father's birthday was coming up, and I wanted to

give him something special. He had always loved playing pool, so without hesitating, I ordered him a billiards table: it only cost a tiny part of our revenue from the week. It would be delivered directly to his house and assembled there. The peak of class. I asked that it be wrapped with a big red ribbon, like in those American TV movies.

On the way home, I stopped at the hairdresser. I'd been wanting to come to this salon for a long time. I had saved photos from the Internet on my phone of the actress Margot Robbie. She was beautiful and elegant — there was something about her. I explained to the hairdresser that I wanted to look like her. Her eyes darted back and forth between the photo and my face. Then the hairdresser covered Margot Robbie's face with her thumb, moved the phone away from her by extending her arm, and closed her right eye. She seemed to be planning the steps; after all, the salon's rates were very high, she was a real professional.

'For the color, that's no problem, you'll have something similar, same for the cut. For the face, though, there's nothing I can do.'

A punch straight to the gut. She had said it so casually that she must not have realized the cruelty of her words. Right away, she led me to the shampoo station and massaged my scalp diligently. No one had ever taken care of me in this way. I was moved.

'Weird, your tips are all stuck together in places, it's like you have gel in your hair.'

SELF-WORTH

It must have been the vestiges of Lulu's vomit. I didn't respond.

After applying a white paste to my locks, she wrapped each strand in aluminum foil, the same kind that I used to store leftover chicken. Then I waited. For a while. I had time to read through the magazines piled up on the coffee table. I learned that to be thin and beautiful, you had to sleep eight hours per night, do an hour of exercise in the morning, not eat sugar, not eat meat, not eat fat, not eat bread or gluten. In short, not eat anything. It was also not recommended to drink tap water, coffee, tea, or soda. Staying out in the sun was a serious mistake, and many young women aren't aware of the consequences. In the background, over the humming of the hairdryers, rich bourgeois women were complaining about their husbands coming back late from work. Do we really need a third second home? At this rate, he'll kill himself before retirement. But yes, on the other hand, it's true that it's quite nice, Cap Ferret. And the real estate industry is booming over there. I preferred the advice of *Marie Claire*. However, against my will, I let myself be caught up in their conversation. I imagined myself as the mistress of a house overlooking the ocean. Lulu, me, my new bag under my arm, my new platinum-blond hair, strolling along the beach for the admiring gazes of passersby, not a trace of Kantian morality on my shoulders.

Once she had cut, dried, brushed, smoothed, and perfumed my hair, the hairdresser turned the chair around so I could see myself in the mirror. I pinched my arm to make sure I wasn't dreaming. I was pretty. Of course, I didn't have Margot Robbie's face, but my features had softened, and the cut made me seem more sophisticated. The hairdresser had earned her hundred and eighty euros. I couldn't wait to show Lulu.

But before going home, I had to take care of several things for our new apartment: we were moving soon. I started by ordering a new bed, because the slats of ours were rotten and Lulu was always postponing when he'd repair them. Then a refrigerator with an ice machine, and a TV so flat it was like a piece of paper. The old TV was going to Emmaüs's place. Each purchase in small bills, of course. I went for the brands with chic names. Ordinarily, my feet would freeze in front of such stores. But I was starting to find my groove. On the way, I gave the equivalent of two or three hundred euros, I can't remember, to a homeless person who thanked me kindly. I walked away with a light heart: I had done a good deed. Energized by this experience, I did the same every time I crossed the path of another homeless person. There were many in our neighborhood. Climbing up the stairwell, I slid some more bills into our neighbors' mailboxes: tax season was coming up.

Lulu jumped when he saw me.

'Who are you and what have you done with my girlfriend?'

'You don't like it?'

SELF-WORTH

'To me, you were just as pretty brunette, but yes, you look very beautiful. If you like it, that's all that matters. Look at all those bags, what did you find for us?'

My arms were full, my pockets empty. A successful outing. I told Lulu everything, with receipts to back it up.

'That's great, but why did you buy a new microwave? Ours works perfectly well.'

'Ah, that's not for us. It's for Bruno on the fourth floor, the same model as his old one.'

'I don't understand, I'm in the middle of fixing it.'

'Exactly! You told me that it's giving you grief; voilà, problem solved! We'll slip him the new one and he'll be none the wiser. I did the same for Bérénice's toaster, Farid's radio, and little Simon's game console. You'll be able to rest, my love, isn't that wonderful?'

Seeing his expression, I understood quickly that no, it was not wonderful.

'But Anna, this is my work. I need to do it.'

'You're not going to keep breaking your back for thirty euros apiece! It's ridiculous, with the money you're making now.'

'And you? You lift your arms up and down all day long for minimum wage. You don't even like your job, but me, I like repairing things.'

'I'm keeping the job as a cover, Thierry told me to. And also to take care of what we can't pay for in cash. If I could, I would stay on the couch all day, too.'

Lulu went quiet. I felt him pulling away from me. Disconcerted, I was searching for the right words when I received a text from Sophie. Bad timing. She was in the middle of completing the written portion of the CAPES and sending me salvos of text messages every day. Her missives varied between 'why did I choose this shitty major', 'I'll never pass', 'I want to kill myself', and 'can you bring me some chocolate ice cream?' At first, I felt sorry for her, but now, it was beginning to get on my nerves. It was always the same story, she never had anything new to say; her life revolved around dead intellectuals that normal people had no desire to hear about. Most of them were already bad company while they were alive, so why was Sophie so persistent? It was so much effort for so little result. She had been warned though, hadn't she? And what about me? Did she wonder for a single second how I was doing, if my job was going well? She was in the ego vortex of exams. I decided to return the favor, and didn't respond.

Vladimir and Estragon called for their meal. While I was feeding the birds, I watched Lulu out of the corner of my eye. He seemed downtrodden. Just as I was thinking he would sulk all night, he suddenly changed his mind.

'I'm sorry, sweetheart. I'm the one who put us in this situation, and you're the one who has to deal with it. I know that you're doing your best, forgive me.'

I hadn't expected that.

'Don't worry about it, Lulu, we're still learning, but with some practice ... All this upheaval is really getting to you. I think we need to take some time for us. I can ask for a few days off. Do you want to go somewhere?'

'Oh, that's a great idea! Dublin? I've always dreamed of going there, and we can take Vladimir and Estragon, it's their ancestral home!'

'Are you kidding? With the money we have, we could go to the end of the world! Let's treat ourselves to a real vacation — a white sand beach, palm trees, cocktails, our toes in the water. We deserve it, don't we?'

8

We could have pulled that super classy move where you point a finger at a random city on the globe and take off, but I was too afraid we'd land on Frankfurt, Bucharest, or even Vierzon. Somewhere ugly and not at all Instagrammable. In the end, we decided, or rather I decided, on Tahiti. I didn't know anything about the culture or what sites to see. To tell the truth, I didn't care. The photos I saw on the Internet were plenty for me. It was far enough away, and coveted enough in the collective imagination, for all my colleagues to say, 'Wow, you're so lucky!' I was beginning to adore it when someone was jealous of me; I drew a particular satisfaction from it. I contacted a travel agency that accepted cash payments. The employees took care of the reservations, hotels and plane tickets included. They proposed an itinerary that consisted of days on the beach punctuated with all-you-can-eat lunch buffets. It was perfect — we were going there precisely to do nothing. The dates were booked for the following month, which left us time to settle into our new apartment.

Thierry's friend had come through. When he brought us there for the first time, we were in awe. The building was located in a single-digit arrondissement. This might not seem a big deal, but it was incredibly chic. The front door opened onto a small passageway that led into a huge living room whose windows offered breathtaking natural light. To the left, the first bedroom. To the right, the second, plus an office, a kitchen, a bathroom and a separate toilet. Solid wood floors, crown moldings, and a fireplace, a real, functional one, not like the pathetic sealed ones I had seen in the chambres de bonnes of my college friends. The finishing touch was a balcony wide enough for a table and chairs. It was so big that, at first, Lulu and I felt lost. For a laugh, we called each other on our cell phones from separate rooms. I hired movers. We chose the Prestige Deluxe service, so we didn't have to do a thing. The company even packed the boxes. Lifting up the gas stove, the guys found a few wads of bills and with integrity handed them over to us, without seeming the least bit surprised. I wasn't sure I would have done the same thing in their place, so to thank them I told them to keep the money. We had to buy new furniture, for the birds, too: bye bye cage and hello aviary, which would allow them to get some exercise.

'It's better, no?'

'It's bigger, but it's still a cage.'

'You're sure you're not the one who studied philosophy?'

Lulu gave me a weird look, without smiling. I guess he hadn't unpacked his sense of humor yet.

We wanted to throw a housewarming party to celebrate our move, but soon I realized we had a space problem: we didn't have enough friends to fill the apartment. Besides, most of them led a life so oppressive that a party risked turning into a psychoanalysis session. Despite my silence, Sophie continued to deluge me with messages, so I cracked and invited her. She had finished the written exams and hadn't yet received the results, an unbearable in-between, a limbo zone where things aren't yet ruined, but they haven't worked out either. It depressed her quite a bit, and she dabbled on forums where other students, as lost as her, compared notes on how they had written their essay on the given topic, 'Do thought experiments allow for a test of alternative approaches of morality?' No one could even agree on what the question meant. So many obscure words, like trying to crack the Rosetta Stone. Élodie couldn't cope with other people's children, and Mehdi, who had quit his fast-food job, was having a hard time finding other work. To brighten up the group, I sent invitations to a few of my coworkers and to a few old acquaintances, classmates I'd lost touch with a long time ago and whose existence, as enriching as it might be, held little interest for me. At least they would take up some space.

Lulu would say he had inherited the apartment from an old uncle, which would spare us any awkward questions. I ordered catered food: smoked salmon at fifteen euros a slice, and bottles of alcohol. Top shelf only. Moët champagne and gin, not strawberry-flavored this time, that was too common. A DJ handled the music, and, for decorations, I had cleaned out Le Bon Marché.

The guests started to arrive, friends from university first, then the work cohort and, finally, a few starlets from the series. The order was important. The cooler you are, the later you arrive. That's why Sophie was the first to ring the bell. She waylaid me for fifteen minutes — the longest quarter of an hour of my life — blathering on about the difference between Cartesian solipsism and the isolation of the individual referred to as Dasein by Heidegger. Who gives a shit? No one. I had a furious desire to scream in her face: *have a glass of champagne, swap that hideous sweater for a little sexy top, and have some fun!* I stifled my yawns with difficulty, but I had a soft spot for her, nonetheless. Sophie was so candid. Fortunately, as she started in on monads, another group of friends showed up. Saved by the bell. I abandoned her to the company of Vladimir and Estragon, who could listen to her unabated.

The ambiance was perfect, and everyone was enjoying themselves. Bursts of laughter. Glasses clinking joyously.

Smell of expensive eau de cologne. Strobe lights. Lulu excused himself every now and then. Handsome in his new clothes. Between dances, the girls dolled ourselves up with glitter and had a photo-shoot. Sandrine wanted to see my walk-in closet. I told her she could help herself. 'You're sure? Wow, thanks, Anna, you're so generous!' Christian charity, no doubt.

I could tell that Mehdi was shocked by the opulence. Between two drinks, he yelled things at me like 'Capital is dead labor that only comes alive by sucking like a vampire from living labor. The more it sucks the more it comes to life,' or 'The wealth of capitalistic societies is evident in the monstrous accumulation of commodities.' In short, hostile and sanctimonious Marxism. He continued by telling me about his problems, the bills he had to pay and all the rest. But I wasn't listening. In his panicked eyes, wet with the anxiety of what lay ahead, I saw only the reflection of my own image. I was stunning. I examined my designer dress and my brand-name lipstick. I was smiling like in a dream. The world was in perfect harmony. The planets were finally aligned.

One of the show's jury members grabbed me by the arm to show me a video on her iPhone 14 of a kitten in a Gucci bag. At first, the closed bag fell over and moved sporadically, then the zipper slowly opened to reveal an adorable little furball. I laughed sincerely then I froze, taken aback. There it was! It had come out so naturally that it seemed unreal:

I finally had the silky laugh of others. A triumph. I had practiced so many times in front of the bathroom mirror. I had done vocal exercises and contorted my mouth in every direction, but it always rang false. Now, for the first time, it had been authentic. A deep laugh, a communion with the elite. I belonged to a group, and not just any group; I had finally become *someone*.

Noticing Mehdi was about to leave, I ran after him into the building courtyard.

'Wait, wait! I wanted to give you something.'

He threw the wad of bills I handed him on the ground as if it were on fire.

'Anna, are you taking the piss? You think I'm some kind of beggar?'

'Don't take it that way, I just wanted to help you ...'

'I don't want your pity. Go back to your fancy apartment with your new fancy friends, and why don't you take that money and gobble it up, choke yourself with it. Do you realize what you've become?'

Lifting my eyes towards the window of our apartment, I saw something like a flash of lightning: the sparklers. I turned around to rejoin the party.

9

We arrived at the Faa'a airport after eighteen hours of flying. The first time in the air for both of us. In first class, of course. Seats shaped like cocoons, the size of a bed, fully reclinable, with a gourmet menu. I was familiar with classic cocktails, the ones that make your head feel good but burn up your stomach. That powerful descaling effect, like a Sex on the Beach — too bitter from the grapefruit. This was a whole other level. For one, the bartender was called a mixologist. A new vocabulary word for us. He squeezed the fruit himself for the original creations he composed based on our first names and our astrological signs. Delicious. The ultimate personalization. The alcohol came from all over the world; we felt like we were landing in Bali at one sip, in Singapore with the next. The meal was cooked by a chef, and I was certain that it was much better than the catered dishes the rich gorged themselves on at work. This gustatory delirium helped us to pass the time. Lulu was stressed; he kept looking out the window and biting his nails.

'Don't worry, if we die, the impact will be so intense you won't feel a thing. Go on, have some chocolate mousse.'

He vomited into a paper bag. Obviously, he couldn't throw it out — it was our money for the taxi — the rest of the bills were in our checked luggage. We had left Vladimir and Estragon at home. A 'birdsitter', as in a babysitter for birds, would go by every day to feed them and play with them.

After we deboarded the plane, a driver in a suit was waiting to take us to the hotel. There were large sweat stains under his armpits. Before we'd even left the airport, I was complaining about the bad WiFi. The two little bars did nevertheless manage to receive a text from Sophie: she had passed the first stage of the exams successfully, and now she had to prepare for her oral exams. I congratulated her quickly, telling her that I was on vacation, that I had been working hard and needed, for once, to take a break. She wrote back: 'Could we Skype so you can help me study remotely?' I ignored it.

'That's not very nice, Anna. The poor thing, she needs you.'

'Is that a joke? Who put up with all the Heraclitus aphorisms for months on end? Was that you?'

Lulu recoiled and dropped my hand. Fine by me, his hand was sweaty anyway.

'Whatever, she's your friend after all.'

SELF-WORTH

The hotel staff greeted us with a welcome cocktail. A kind of orangeade topped with a candy skewer. This tackiness aside, the place was magnificent. A five-star hotel, good value for the money. I trusted what the brochure said because, never having stayed at a hotel, I had no point of comparison. A woman in traditional clothing brought us to our bungalow with a straw roof, overlooking the sea. I watched her pareo flutter elegantly. The room smelled like vanilla, and must have been twice the size of our old apartment. The air conditioner was set to our preferences, which I had indicated beforehand in a very detailed form. This form also allowed us to choose a superior mattress, neither too hard nor too soft. And I'd asked for bamboo toothpicks, just for the fun of it. The towels were folded in the shape of two swans in love; fresh fruit was displayed in a magnificent basket. On the outdoor terrace was a jacuzzi and robes embroidered with our initials.

'Isn't this a bit much?' Lulu worried, visibly uncomfortable.

'What's rare is expensive, as Plato said.'

'Clearly you have no shame.'

I was too busy fiddling with the pressure of the tub jets to respond.

The beginning of the trip passed without a hitch. There was unlimited bar access, and Tahitian women brought us whatever we wanted, directly to our beach chairs. The buffet was amazing, delicate dishes made from sophisticated ingredients: scallops with caviar, Tournedos Rossini, sea bream crusted with Himalayan salt and gold leaf for some color, Ladurée macarons flown from Paris on a jet that very morning. The water wasn't exactly the same color as what I'd seen on Google but, with a few filters, the result was similar. At night, there was a show over dinner, fire breathers and other dances. I found it folkloric and quite charming, despite the unbelievable racket of the drums.

Everything was ruined on the morning of the third day. Lulu wanted to eat 'something simple' — the refined dishes were irritating his stomach. He wanted an egg, for fuck's sake, it wasn't rocket science. I told him to calm down, I would see what I could do. I found the Tahitian woman in charge of breakfast and explained my problem. She listened to me carefully, repeating 'egg OK egg OK egg OK'. I was worried she was having a stroke. Not long after, a server hurried over to Lulu and deposited a plate with a beautiful fried egg in the middle.

'What are those little black spots?'
'It must be pepper. You see, you got your egg!'
'It's truffles. I can't believe it!'

He took off angry, leaving his plate untouched. I found

his reaction a bit excessive. The egg yolk stared back at me confused.

Towards the beginning of the afternoon, while we were lying peacefully in the sun, Lulu started to dump loads of information about Tahiti on me. Surface area of 1,042 square kilometers. The biggest and most populated of all the French Polynesian islands. Economic activity primarily from the service industry. Scars of successive colonizations. Blah blah blah. Then he announced that he wanted to go on a hike or visit the Robert Wan Pearl Museum. In short, he had totally lost it.

'Why do you want to walk around for hours in the blazing sun when we're so comfortable here?'

'I'm sick of seeing nothing. Beach–restaurant. Beach–jacuzzi. Beach–pool. It's ridiculous, we haven't learned anything about the country.'

'You're forgetting the cultural performances, my kitten.'

'You call that culture? It's for the tourists, there's no authenticity. I'm going; you can stay here if you want.'

I simply moved my head into the shade with a detached smile. It would soon be four o'clock, the perfect time to post a photo on social media. Thanks to Sandrine's advice, I had doubled my followers. And she commented on all my posts with 'So cool, Anna!' or 'It's so ugly in Paris,' or 'The guys look like total babes'. Since I had stopped answering her texts and calls, Sophie had started to comment on my posts, too. Under the photo of a palm tree, she wrote:

'Anna, for Bergson, the movement of life is indivisible or undivided? Help me plz I'm so lost. I have my oral soon.' I systematically suppressed my shame.

My goal wasn't to become an influencer, but I liked the idea of people liking me. As everyone does. After a few tries, I found the perfect angle for a selfie. My phone sixty centimeters away from my face, arm curved at an 85-degree angle. Quite the contortion. From the outside, it must have looked pretty strange, but the result was fantastic. Just as I was taking the photo, I bit the inside of my cheeks. It made me look thinner, and gave my face a serious and melancholic expression. Digital philosopher of the twenty-first century. And among my new followers? Adam Lesieur: bull's-eye. I reveled in the pathetic and poorly framed photos on his profile. His pavillon in the suburbs, his work as a speech therapist, his stay-at-home-mom wife and her mouthwatering apple tarts, his English Springer Spaniel, his first son, his premature balding, his Friday night badminton classes. In sum: his shitty life. He sent me a message: 'Wow, Anna, what a transformation. You've really changed!' I purposely positioned my head between the sun-drenched beach and my overpriced cocktail and took a selfie. I sent it to him with the caption, 'up your's'. 'Uh, not so different after all, apparently! It's spelled "yours".' He could go fuck himself for all I cared.

I was coming out of my massage when a blonde woman, whose age I couldn't guess because of the Botox, approached me. She had noticed me during breakfast and found me charming. She wanted us to have dinner together — her husband, Lulu, and me — that night. Plus, we were platinum-blonde hair sisters! I was flattered that someone so elegant had taken an interest in me. I adopted a high-pitched voice to confirm that we'd be there, table 239, right by the fountain. 'Better the sound of the fake waterfall than those awful drums.' I couldn't have agreed more. She put her Gucci sunglasses back on and gave me an 'air kiss', without her voluptuous lips touching my cheek even a little bit. Then she walked along the pool, trailed by her tiny dog; it was a puny chihuahua but, like its mistress, displayed its pedigree proudly.

'You're sure you want to go in your swimming trunks?'

I scrutinized Lulu with a critical eye. It was a way of saying: *Definitely do not go in your swimming trunks.*

'Oh who cares, it's just dinner, and we don't even know these people! Besides, they kind of seem like snobs, don't you think?'

'So what? Don't embarrass me, please, at least put on some pants.'

He put on a pair of jeans while I was turning my suitcase inside out looking for my chicest outfit. Fortunately, to be on the safe side, I'd brought several satin dresses.

Veronica and her husband were sipping glasses of white

wine. When she noticed us, she waved with incredible grace. She was holding her dog in her other arm. Philippe introduced himself and apologized for having his nose glued to his phone. 'The stock market ...' he said in a whisper. We ordered appetizers: oysters, salmon, 'and caviar!' demanded Veronica. 'We're on vacation, after all!'

We cheers'ed to the good life and the yachts polluting the ocean but oh well, we won't be around anymore to see the planet implode. Lulu didn't speak, but seemed fascinated by the fact that the chihuahua had a dish cooked specially for him. Philippe checked his email.

'My husband works a lot, excuse him. He doesn't know how to take a break.'

'I work in M&A, it's true, but we also have my mother's inheritance.'

'In what?' Lulu asked.

'Mergers and acquisitions. Anyway, that's not very interesting. Lulu, what's your profession?'

'I repair objects.'

'Ah! So you're an engineer. I've always respected that kind of work. You need rigor, discipline, and such inventiveness!'

'No, no, I just repair objects. Like a handyman.'

I kicked him hard under the table. Seeing Philippe's confusion, I tried to divert the couple's attention.

'And you, Veronica? Let me guess, you're a model, right?'

'Hahaha, you're very sweet, Anna. No, I don't have time to work, little Grégoire takes up all my energy ...'

'You have a son?' Lulu asked.

'A child? God no, this is Grégoire.'

She lifted her chihuahua who, his mouth still full of crab, started to lick her face. Lulu put down his fork and looked away.

'You don't want kids, Anna, do you?'

'We haven't talked about it, to tell the truth, but I ...'

'Definitely don't do it, your body after ... The horror! You've seen them, all those women full of stretch marks around the pool, right? Honestly, we deserve better than that.'

She touched my hand with a knowing expression. Veronica wasn't wrong. She asked me what I did for work. I stammered.

'I'm a stylist, well, I do a lot of things, but fashion, it's not really a job, it's more of a passion.'

'What are you talking about?' Lulu whispered.

Reproach oozed from his eyes, and his face was twisted into his classic expression of disappointment. I wasn't about to confess to Veronica that our fortune came from his stomach and that I spent the whole day lifting my arms up and down like a robot.

'How wonderful!' (I don't know whether Veronica was talking about fashion design or the stuffed shark that had just been placed on the table.) 'It's clear immediately,

Anna, that you're not one of those women who dresses in those awful ready-to-wear brands. You realize that it's children who make those clothes, somewhere in China? It's shameful. But let's not talk about tragic things, there's so much beauty in the universe.'

Philippe agreed while tapping away on his phone. Grégoire was having a field day, gradually licking off Veronica's makeup. A few brownish spots emerged from beneath her foundation.

'Well, dear Anna, there's something I've been wanting to ask you since I first saw you ... Maybe it's too invasive, but ... are those your real cheekbones? They're so prominent, it's incredible. I NEED the name of your surgeon.'

I was delighted; my ego inflated like a balloon ready to explode.

'Sorry to disappoint you, Veronica, but, yes, these are my real cheekbones. Yours are also stunning.'

'These ridiculous nubs? You're kidding! I have one wish: to have them redone.'

'I'd love to get my nose done,' I confessed.

Lulu spat out his glass of wine. A few droplets spattered Philippe's phone, but he remained unperturbed.

'Anna, you're not serious! You can't risk going under the knife for no reason! Your nose is lovely.'

'Hey ho, young man!' Veronica interrupted. 'Does women's liberation mean anything to you? We don't need your permission. What's next, we can't have a checkbook or a bank account in our name? The patriarchy is over.'

Lulu stayed quiet. Perhaps because he was shocked that I wanted to have plastic surgery, but perhaps because Veronica had used the term 'patriarchy' in a way that only she understood.

Despite his chronic muteness, Philippe felt the atmosphere tense. By way of reconciliation, he offered to teach Lulu how to play golf. It's a great sport to take a load off. But Lulu left the table before dessert. His loss, the Baked Alaska was delicious. Veronica and I continued talking and I was impressed by her specific tastes, her good breeding. I could learn a thing or two from her. I got her phone number. They lived between New York and Copacabana, but, of course, had a little pied-à-terre in Paris; just one phone call, and the plane would drop her off in time for brunch!

Lulu didn't come back until well after midnight, stinking of sweat and leaving piles of dirt in the shower. Fortunately, the cleaner could be called twenty-four hours a day. I needed money for the next day; I was planning to buy myself some new bathing suits at the hotel boutique. Between the pareos, the tips for the young women who fanned us with palm leaves on our beach chairs, and the dozens of cloth bracelets I'd bought so the beach vendor would finally leave us alone, there were almost no bills left in the suitcase. I turned the entire bungalow upside down, but I couldn't find any more cash and, thinking about it, I realized I hadn't seen Lulu vomit once since we'd arrived.

'No, I haven't coughed up anything since the plane,' he confirmed.

'What are we going to do now?'

'I don't know, Anna, it'll be okay. We still have a bit of cash, it should last us.'

'And my bathing suits?'

'Do you really need them? You haven't even asked me how my day was ...'

'If you stuck your finger down your throat, do you think that would work?'

He called me crazy, and I sulked. Eventually I wore him down and he gave in. It still didn't work.

'You're not putting them down far enough, let me do it.'

I didn't leave him time to protest. I buried my index and middle fingers down to his glottis. He heaved. Not enough. He tried to get away, but I held him down firmly. I tried again, scratching a bit with my nail. Then he vomited. When he lifted his head, his gaze had changed. Much more somber. I could tell there was something brewing inside of him, and it wasn't a flood of cash. He was angry, an expression I rarely saw on his face. I caressed his forehead and summoned all the tenderness I could muster to murmur: 'Thank you.' I was relieved, until I noticed that in the toilet bowl were not the usual blue bills, but two-euro coins.

'Alright, are you happy now?'

'What do you expect me to do with this change? This isn't enough, what a nightmare.'

'Are you ever going to worry about me, Anna? Like people who love each other?'

'I'm worried about you, of course I am, what are you talking about? But you said it yourself, it's nothing serious.'

'My body is now producing coins. It's full of iron. I've lost eight kilos and I'm starting to lose my teeth. I could die from this, and you, all you can think about is your fucking bathing suits.'

'You could die? Isn't that a bit of an exaggeration?'

He slammed the door on his way out for a night pirogue ride, or some other absurd activity, and left me all alone.

Clearly, I had to forget about my bathing suits. The obligatory expenses of our trip — food, room, and beach chairs — had been paid for in advance, but I had to be careful with the extras. Bye bye, coconut oil massages from soft, expert hands. We tightened our belts, and the rest of our vacation was fine. To apologize, I even followed Lulu on one of his outings. 'Isn't it amazing?' he said in front of the tombstones of some population decimated ages ago. 'Yes, yes, incredible, but still, so much space dedicated to the dead … they could have built a beautiful resort with a big pool here, it's south facing.'

———

I paid the taxi while Lulu brought the bags up to our apartment. When I opened the door, it was dark; he hadn't turned the light on. I saw him crouched in the middle of the living room on the alpaca rug. Lulu was sobbing his eyes out and holding something against his chest. Then he gently unfolded himself, like a piece of crumpled paper. He was babbling a strange language. Full of suffering. Torn expression that seemed to reopen the wounds inside his cheeks. Unintelligible. Hoarse, animal cries. Snot. Drool. Sniffling. A torrent. Eventually he extended his left hand, palm opened to the sky. Estragon was resting on his fingers. Stiff and cold. He even tried a desperate mouth-to-mouth CPR under the panic-stricken eyes of Vladimir who didn't understand what was happening. Lulu and his drowned gaze. I was grieving, not for the sparrow, but for my boyfriend.

Lulu's muscles tensed when I tried to take the bird.

'You're not going to throw him in the trash, are you? Don't throw him out, Anna, please.'

'Why are you crying, Lulu? It's no big deal, we'll buy another.'

He stared at me with disgust.

'You're a monster.'

Tears were streaming down his face into the wells of his dimple. It was inundated. The comma had become a period. I rubbed his shoulder. He lurched away from me. I was finally able to take the bird into my hands. A green feather fell to the ground. I put Estragon in a plastic bag and then placed him in the freezer. No more frozen meals for us. No matter, it had been a long time since we'd eaten one of those.

10

I had no desire to go back to work the next day. I'd heaped loads of affectionate comfort and attention on Lulu, who had basically not slept the entire night. He couldn't stop writhing all over the place. His body was eating away at him uncontrollably; he scratched himself till he bled. This despite the fact that our sheets were hypoallergenic satin. I concluded that he was in a psychosomatic delirium, like those people who end things with their partner and then go to a doctor complaining of heart failure. That had always seemed a bit far-fetched to me, but Lulu was really suffering, so why not.

I arrived at the studio late, with huge sunglasses, the size of two fists, to mask my under-eye circles. Everyone was silent. I hurried into an empty chair. On my way people complimented me: 'Nice tan', 'You got so dark.' I sat next to Sandrine, who was squeezing a new purse against her chest and pulling at the sleeves of her sweater to hide her forearms. I noticed bruises and what seemed like scratches. 'The stairs,' she said, repeating the movement of her shoulders that signified her absent-mindedness.

Bertrand and Marc looked very serious. Recently, people on the Internet had become enraged. The reason: the booing of certain comedians by the studio audience. The spectators found it degrading, animalistic. It wasn't the 1990s anymore, television should be benevolent. Amusement without acerbity. The same went for some of the contestants' bits that were deemed too divisive. Even though the show didn't air on a public channel, it should still aim for a family-friendly vibe. Production had ignored these reprimands until the trickles turned into a tidal wave. Bertrand himself was criticized for his remarks, which were deemed awful. He was reproached for encouraging hate. Quick quick, restore the image. Crisis management meeting. No soul-searching, just Band-Aids. Anna, no more boos, understood? Eliminate one of your three standard gestures. A life coach for Bertrand. Sack the person who writes the teleprompter text. Get rid of the contestants who use dark humor. Sandrine, for the next taping, try to put two or three disabled people and fat moms in the first row, okay? And voilà. Case closed. The farce could continue.

Thierry paid me a discreet visit before the recording started. While I was on vacation, he'd been working hard.

SELF-WORTH

He revealed a shady plan involving one of his friends who worked at a kebab shop in the suburbs of Paris, ideal for our needs — we just had to invest in a small business like that. The world might crumble, but people will always be hungry, so there's no real risk. I had trouble imagining how meat could be enough to launder so much money. But it didn't matter; we didn't have any more. I was nervous to tell him that we had to give up on our ruse. I said something about supply issues. Thierry, clearly experienced, answered that he understood, that I just had to get back in touch with him when the machine was operational again.

The rest of the day was one of the most difficult I'd had there. I was overcome by an unpleasant sensation: laziness. Same sequence — arms, laughter, arms, applause. The laughs that escaped from those free mouths bothered me more and more. I found them coarse, crude, trivial. I wanted them to stop, I needed a moment of peace. So, I started spacing out my signals. Marc soon came to put me back in my place. One, two, three times before telling me that I had to pick up the pace if I wanted to keep my job, that anyone could fill my role. He'd just have to put an ad online and in less than thirty minutes an enthusiastic young woman would come to take my place. I lowered my eyes like a chastised child and suffered in silence until the end of the recording.

Back at home, I found Lulu in his swimming trunks in the bathroom. I approached him gently; like a loving girlfriend, I'd bought him anti-itch cream. His torso was stained with greenish spots. Had he fallen down the stairs? He asked me to examine him. From a distance, it looked like wounds but as I approached, I saw something like a watermark beneath the surface.

'Fuck, Lulu, I can't believe it, it's a hundred-euro bill.'
'What?'

Distressed, he took his head in his hands and hid his eyes, which had become very green again. His mouth contorted downwards into a mournful expression. Under his skin, the right corner of the bill was folded down, peeking out slightly. I tried pulling on it.

'What are you doing?'
'It's like a Band-Aid, I think. You have to yank it off in one go, so it doesn't hurt as much.'
'You're insane, you're going to flay me!'

Despite his protests, pulling out the bill seemed like the right thing to do. I was careful to keep it intact, but it wasn't easy. The epidermis above resisted. Lulu's skin had become elastic, and the membrane surrounding the paper stretched without breaking. When I finally managed to extract the bill, a few drops of blood spurted onto the mirror. In its place was now a sort of suntan with deep holes in the four corners. Nothing dramatic, it would fade in a few days.

'Not so bad, see!'

'Yeah right, look how much it's bleeding.'

Two small tears pearled at the corners of his eyes. Poor man who had never known the pain of getting waxed. I, on the other hand, was thrilled. For the last few days, I'd been afraid that we were poor again. The thought was unbearable to me. Before removing the other bills from him, as a precaution, I repeated my little game at the bar-tabac to verify that the bill was real. All the stores in our new neighborhood had point-of-sale machines, the latest no-contact technology, to the extent that cash had become obsolete. So, I took a taxi; I trusted only Christelle. Stepping foot back in my old arrondissement made me break out in a cold sweat. I entered the bar, and the anise smell of spilled pastis made me dry heave. Christelle didn't recognize me, but she was categoric, the bill was authentic. Before opening the cash register, she said:

'But for a Coke and chewing gum, I can't take such a big bill. I have almost no cash.'

I was already outside.

When I got home, Lulu had his sweater on again.

'There's no way you're removing the rest, it hurts too much.'

'Lulu, we need that money to pay rent, and besides, you can't just hang around with those bills stuck to your body, that's ridiculous.'

'Easy for you to say, you're not the one being skinned!'

'Come on, you can do it!'

The session lasted for a while. I put on classical music to cover up Lulu's screams. Like a pig being slaughtered. A crime scene. I was afraid that our neighbors would call the police. In the end, the harvest was quite satisfactory: twenty bills in total. Lulu stored them in a coffee tin that he placed on a high kitchen shelf.

'Can you pass me one? For the taxi tomorrow, to go to work.'

'I thought we were trying to save, Anna. It's not going to last forever, all this.'

'So, what? You don't want me to take the RER, do you?'

He gave me two bills and made me promise that it would cover all my expenses for the week. Then he put a padlock on the tin and hid the key. I felt humiliated, a little girl being deprived of her treat. I tried to get around it, like the conniving kids on the school playground who steal other people's afternoon snacks. The rest of the night, I was on my best behavior. Waited on him hand and foot. I hadn't touched a pan in weeks, but I cooked a special meal, chicken with asparagus in a pepper sauce. The result was pretty disappointing, a brown mixture that called to mind Lulu's vomit. But for him, it was the thought that counted. After dinner, I massaged him, trying discreetly to loosen a bill or two, but the oil made his skin too slippery. We had sex, pornographic moans and acrobatic moves for good measure. Exuberant orgasm: Palme d'Or at Cannes. He was delighted. I hoped that after such a display of devotion, he would remove the padlock, but Lulu was no fool, no sir!

Obviously, within twelve hours, I had spent all my cash. Not a cent left, bankrupt. I tried to call him on his cell phone so that he could replenish me, but Lulu ignored my calls. Back at the apartment after work — I was forced to take public transport — I hurled myself at the tin. I grabbed a pair of pliers to break the padlock, I jumped on it with both feet hoping to buckle the metal. Nothing worked. Out of options, I tried to make myself vomit, too. After all, it had happened to Lulu, why not me? I sniffed the communal trash; I ate expired fish; I even tried sticking two fingers down my throat. I managed a few secretions, but nothing conclusive. I was spent, in all senses of the term. The situation couldn't have been more catastrophic. Forty-five minutes later, Lulu came back from the supermarket, his arms full of the off-brand products I used to buy before, which now disgusted me.

'I'm not touching that.'

'Alright, you don't have to eat then. Come on, Anna, grow up.'

Once the groceries were put away, he returned to his task. Recently, he had started repairing objects again. I watched those gestures that had so impressed me before, but which now inspired only contempt. Meanwhile, I flipped through a magazine that detailed the outfits of celebrities at the latest Met Gala, trying to concentrate despite the noise of the sander. I drifted off into fantasies about Brad Pitt and Joaquin Phoenix — at least they didn't have dirty hands stained with wood glue.

Lulu cracked jokes to try to cheer me up. When I came out of the shower, he stood before me with his face covered by Jason Statham's, which he had cut out of my magazine. 'Sorry I'm not more like him, but maybe I could get similar muscles …' It touched me deep in my heart. The beating knocked in my chest again. Teary eyes. Budding desire in the hollow of my loins. Real desire, this time. I believed in it. It had come back. We had grown distant, but everything was possible once more. I ran my hands through his hair and promised that never again would I try to rip money out of his back. We heated up the oven and ate a frozen pizza while watching a movie. I leaned my head on his shoulder. The rustling of the paper made a pleasant sound.

11

I did my best, I swear. I concentrated all my energy into being satisfied with a daily life made up of Rosette sausage sandwiches and Saturday mornings at the movie theater before sunrise for the discounted tickets. I strove to enjoy the synthetic clothing that cost less than twenty euros apiece. I tried to revel in free activities such as 'strolling' and reading. I even dipped back into *Capital*, which had been serving as a wedge for the Louis XV dressing table I'd found at an auction. During my sleepless nights, I forced myself not to think of the money sleeping peacefully in the padlocked coffee tin and growing in vain under Lulu's skin. Despite all these efforts, life seemed as insipid as surimi sticks.

The withdrawal was rough. Lulu replenished me from time to time so that I could buy a little trinket to lift my spirits. But it was never enough. To calm me down, he told me to find my inner child, to get back in touch with my roots, and all that bullshit you read in self-help books. On that note, I had thirty-four missed calls from my father. I hadn't meant to ignore them, I'd just been too busy. Maybe Lulu was right — I had nothing to lose by paying him a visit.

My dad opened the door, and I was hit with a blast of sugar and butter straight to my nostrils. I hugged him, and it was as if I'd put on lip balm, so shiny with grease was his cheek.

'I'm just finishing the crepes and then I'm all yours!'

Leaning over the stove, dish towel on his shoulder, my father slid the little disc of batter and flipped it with an agility I recognized well. His back was less upright than in my childhood, he was less quick on his feet, but his essence was still there. I leaned against the doorframe and, gazing across the room, I noticed a photocopy of my master's diploma, stuck to the fridge with one of those free magnets in the shape of a region of France that's included inside mass-produced ham and cheese escalopes. I lifted the folded corner of the paper. Some ketchup had dried on the surface.

'Why do you still have this, Papa? You can throw it out, it's worthless.'

'Oh, Anna, just because you've moved into a new field doesn't mean you should disown your past. You should be proud of yourself.'

The crepe was starting to burn in the pan.

'Shit,' my dad said. 'Go sit down, I'll join you in a minute.'

The apartment had basically not changed at all, and nor had he. Of course, the walls had yellowed, the plaster was crumbling in certain places, in the corners especially, but if you didn't look too closely, it wasn't offensive. Even so, I felt a vague unease; disgust gradually climbed from my stomach to tap the lump in the hollow of my throat like a pool cue. There it was, proudly presiding over the living room. It seemed much bigger than when I'd bought it, likely because the room was narrower than the store. The pool table seemed never to have been used.

'You don't play, Papa?'

Over the spluttering of the pan, I heard him say, slightly embarrassed:

'Oh, I do, but you know, it's not as fun on your own ...'

I chose to ignore this. I continued my exploration of his apartment, like a museum of the working class with all its kitsch and disrepair. I was ashamed. The collection of snow globes depicting countries he'd never been to languished on a shelf; the large painting of a New York taxi bought at Gifi hung over the dresser. I had an idea that brought the smile back to my face.

'Papa, what if we went to the United States? I'll pay for the hotel, the flight, all of it, first class!'

My dad laughed. He returned from the kitchen with a mountain of crepes and placed them on the coffee table, which was covered by a waxed tablecloth.

'That's a funny idea, sweetheart. What would I do in the United States? Rodeo?'

'You could see something new, a change of scenery.'

'I have no need, Anna, we already live in the most beautiful city in the world!'

I picked at my cuticles. He was so narrow-minded ... I remembered the day we'd moved into this apartment. My father had lied a little on our application, doctored his pay stubs so that the real estate agent and the owners wouldn't cringe. We didn't know anyone who made enough money to be our guarantor in case of unpaid rent, so my father had crossed his fingers tight, full of hope. He came home one night, so happy, and lifted me in his arms: 'We did it, Anna, we're going to live in Paris! In the heart of the world, the place to be.' Like a teenager who'd been invited to his first party. I didn't understand why it was so important to him. I had my friends in the neighborhood, my pink Kiabi overalls, and my two incisors had just fallen out, giving me an exuberant gap-toothed smile: I was already happy. We packed up our boxes, and even though all we had to do was cross le Périph to reach this paradise on earth, for my father, this journey was the equivalent of a long-distance flight. That morning, he had put on a suit and tie, repeating in front of the mirror, 'We're moving to the capital, after all!' Then he'd combed my hair for several minutes and helped me into a pretty dress: 'We have to show them we're not hicks!' Once we arrived in the small one-bedroom apartment (to give me some privacy, he would sleep on the living room couch), he took my hand and led me to the window.

'So, what do you think?'

'I don't know, it's just a street.'

'Don't ever say that again, Anna. You know, there are many very important people who have walked on this street, like Mitterrand or Johnny Hallyday.'

When he spoke on the phone to our former neighbors in Bobigny, he insisted that we had a view of the Eiffel Tower. Geographically, that was impossible, but no one dared point that out. In a supermarket next to our new apartment, he had found the same brand of chicken that we were used to eating every Sunday.

'Isn't this better than back home?'

So, Paris wasn't really home. The City of Light would remain an elsewhere and us its enthusiastic squatters, dazzled by the largesse of its sidewalks and the history of its monuments.

'You could visit the Empire State Building and lounge in luxury hotels!' I suggested, emerging from my memories.

'Oh, that's not really my thing...'

'What is your thing, then? Discount coupons and old reruns on TV?'

I immediately regretted my jab. My father looked

down. I had hurt him, but I couldn't help it.

'Alright, let's drop it! Have a crepe, darling.'

'Thanks, but I'm not hungry.'

'One of your favorite cookies then? I always have some in the kitchen in case you come by.'

'Cookies are also food, and I said I'm not hungry.'

'Okay, okay, a coffee then?'

Before I could answer, he was back in the kitchen. I stayed seated on the couch, which had always been covered in plastic, because my father didn't want to ruin it. He'd bought it twelve years ago.

'You still use a French press? Come on, Papa, I'll order you a real coffee maker, a Nespresso, you'll see, there's no comparison.'

'Thank you, but I like my French press.'

I had already pulled out my phone to order him a coffee maker on Amazon. With Prime, it would be delivered the next day.

'What are you doing? You finally come to visit, you could at least put away your phone ...'

'I'm buying you a new coffee maker, just a sec.'

Unexpectedly, my phone was smacked out of my hand and landed on the carpet.

'Are you crazy? What's your problem?'

'Sorry, sweetie,' my father said, slightly distraught, 'it's just that ... Stop trying to buy me things. I just want to spend time with you.'

SELF-WORTH

I didn't listen to his apology. I was already headed for the door.

'Wait, wait, Anna, I'll wrap up some crepes for you to take to Lulu, maybe he'll be hungry. And you haven't told me about your trip, was it nice?'

I heard his voice resound in the stairwell. He caught up to me on the sidewalk.

'I appreciate all you're trying to do for me, forgive me, kiddo. A hug at least? Come back and see me again soon, promise?'

Once I'd left the neighborhood, I could breathe again. I asked the taxi driver for hand sanitizer. If I could have, I would have covered my entire body with it. I felt so grimy.

'Did you have a nice time with your dad?' Lulu asked me.

'Super. He says hi, by the way.'

For a few days, I had a hard time getting up in the morning, going to work became a crucible. I was a depressed puppet whose strings had to be pulled to lift its arms. With nothing new to show off for my colleagues, I went unnoticed, a nobody again. So, without telling Lulu, I invented excuses not to go to work when I felt too disheartened to show up. A broken water heater, a sick child to look after at home (I didn't have a kid, of course, but this detail didn't occur to anyone). The minor inconveniences of normal people. Marc would complain over the phone but eventually give in; Sandrine was perfectly capable of standing in for me for a day.

Thus liberated, I spent my time in luxury boutiques. The saleswomen, whom I had come to know, greeted me warmly. Sometimes, I enjoyed trying on the new dresses, aware that I could no longer buy them. That's what my existence amounted to now: a series of frustrations.

However, in front of Lulu, I didn't let any of this show. These sacrifices were for his sake. He certainly didn't realize the extent of it, making fun of my growing malaise. Our love, on the other hand, was like the first days again. He looked at me tenderly and kindly, rubbed my feet when I took a nap. My comfort.

But one night, I couldn't contain myself. Lulu had undressed to get in bed. On his back, the bills were like little scales. There were bills of all amounts and colors. A multicolored shell. Mythological beast with iridescent gleams. Beautiful. Powerful. Stronger than ever before. I wanted to lick this new skin. Kneel down at the feet of this demigod. Pledge to him my eternal allegiance. Give myself as an offering. Fascinated and frenzied. The power of imagination became irresistible: I was soaking wet. Lulu got aroused seeing the effect he had on me. He kissed me while I bit him. His hands traveled down between my legs, his cock entered me. We acted out Plato's 'Androgyne'.

Soulmates who had finally found each other again. No longer two distinct bodies, but a single, indivisible one. He moved faster and faster, and I got carried away, too. I groped his arms, which were hardened by the money. I was enveloped, snug. Then, with a mind of their own, my fingers started to scratch. I was surprised by my anxious, erratic gestures. My thumb and index fingers drew together like a pincer and grabbed hold of one of the bills. My muscles tensed; I yanked it with all my strength. The bill was too firmly stuck. Lulu didn't notice: he took it for a fit of passion. So, I picked a more strategic placement, just to the right of his spine, near the nape of his neck. I disguised my attempts by also rubbing him in other places, but this time, the ruse didn't last. When I used enough force to rip out a hundred-euro bill, Lulu started. He recoiled brusquely, his face shiny with sweat.

'Are you skinning me again? You need help, you're scaring me.'

'I'm sorry, I'm sorry, my love. I didn't mean to ...'

'It's over, Anna, you've gone way too far this time.'

Lulu turned his back to me and covered himself with the duvet. I took a sleeping pill to suppress my sadness and worry, hoping that by the morning he would have forgiven me. A bump in the road. That was all.

That night, I had an incredible dream. I was sailing on a river in a small boat with wooden oars. Thirsty, I leaned over the canoe. I formed a small cup with my hands to collect water and, when I brought them to the surface, they were filled with money. The river was offering me an inexhaustible source. I swallowed the bills. Fistfuls of them. I was stuffed with happiness. Finally satisfied. I brushed the bills over my neck and thighs. I rubbed them around inside my underwear. It was more erotic than anything I'd felt before. I was tireless, a bottomless well. The bills slid down my throat without the slightest difficulty.

When I woke up, I reflexively stretched my arm to the right but felt only the sheets. Opening my eyes, I saw that in Lulu's place was nothing but a five-euro bill. I jumped up. My light steps creaked along the floor. I peered into the second bedroom, the living room, the bathroom. I looked out the window to inspect the balcony. I even rummaged around the bottom of the dirty laundry. Lulu was nowhere to be found.

I scrutinized the bill in the bedroom. A shred of skin was still stuck to the back. I was gripped by panic. What if I had really done it? What if my dream wasn't a dream? What if I had skinned Lulu down to nothing? I tried to be sensible. It was impossible, after all — a human body would leave something behind. A substratum. Bones, at least. Lulu couldn't have transformed into a pile of cash with nothing beneath it but air. Still, plausibility had abandoned us long ago. Unless ... he had left? I opened the closets: his things were still arranged in their usual place. I waited a few hours, in case he came back. I called him fifteen times. I left him incoherent voicemails — 'My love, are you okay? Call me back, please', then 'You asshole, answer me!' — before realizing that his cell phone was wedged in the couch. My panic cranked up a notch. The lump was getting heavier and heavier. The weight of it made me fall to the floor.

At the end of a day of nail-biting and nervous knee-jiggling, I finally decided to retrieve the coffee tin. I hoisted myself onto a stepladder and reached my hand as far as it could go, blindly groping the top of the highest shelf. I managed to graze the edge of the metal object and, with a sweeping gesture, finally knocked the tin down. The padlock had been removed, the money with it.

While Vladimir watched me pace back and forth across the apartment, which now seemed so empty, I thought back to the events of the past few months, like in the movies when a flashback flits rapidly in the mind of the main character. Images passed by, sometimes superimposed on each other. Our happy memories of flying paper airplanes into the Seine, afternoons spent loving each other. I was emotional. Then an idea hit me right in the face: somewhere between our first date to the movies and the last time I'd worn cashmere, a word from Lulu slipped in, casually, which now took on its full meaning. If he had left, he could only be in one place, and I was going to bring him back by the scruff of his neck. No one abandoned me like this. Especially not without a penny. I had the answer.

12

Before leaving, I checked my bank account to assess the situation. I had just about enough money to buy myself a baguette. I had spent my entire salary and couldn't remember on what. In order to pay for my Lulu search, with a heavy heart, I sold objects that I no longer needed on Leboncoin. Potential buyers quibbled over a few cents, noting the scuff mark on the calfskin leather boots, the slightly stuck pushbutton on the iPad. Alright, do you want it or not? We can't go back and forth all night. I accepted the discounts they demanded, I needed the money. At first, I had trouble letting go of my things; my fingers tensed, clutched the fabric. Then, gradually, watching these old things disappear gave me a certain lightness. Designer lamps and alarm clocks, name-brand skirts and handbags were borne away in the basket of a bicycle, heading for another apartment where they would illuminate, wake up, and clothe people who weren't me. I wished them godspeed.

I bought a ticket from a budget airline. My carbon footprint? Our generation had already made the enormous sacrifice of plastic straws in fast-food restaurants. Everything in its own time. This airline offered discounts galore, flashy colors to drum up business, dream destinations for ridiculous prices. That said, you had to pay to choose your seat, pay for a plug to charge your devices, pay to have a large suitcase or a small one, pay to drink water. And to bring the bird, same deal. Upcharge upcharge upcharge. So, I left with a light backpack and layers of clothes piled on my body. I checked the weather. In Paris, summer was approaching, but over there it was arctic cold. Climate change, no doubt. I didn't mind — I wanted to disappear under the wool, bury myself beneath my scarf. I wouldn't recharge my phone, and I would leave my seat to chance. I didn't need to drink water, anyway.

The Beauvais airport was located outside the city. Far, very far in fact. Farther than the end of the RER D line. I didn't think that was possible. It was out of the question to call a taxi, as we had when Lulu and I left for Tahiti. I had to take a shuttle. Alarm set for four in the morning. A fright in front of the bathroom mirror. Eyes puffy, swollen, ready to explode. Face like someone exhumed. Lips dry like I was hungover. Vladimir was silent. The final flowers given to me by Lulu, which I hadn't been able to throw out, were completely withered. The roses drooped sadly towards the floor. The green foam that had formed on the water's surface emitted a moldy odor. An abandoned funeral parlor. I put the five-euro bill — the last trace of Lulu — in my pocket, for luck. I closed the door and left Vladimir in this tomb with enough seeds to wage a war.

It was still dark when I arrived at the parking lot. The lit cigarettes seemed frozen in space, little stars. Constellation of the poor. The bus doors finally opened. Right away, I noticed that the majority of passengers had opted for the same strategy as me: layers and layers of clothing that they hadn't bothered to remove because, sooner or later, they'd have to put them back on. They tugged at their turtlenecks, faces sweating. Their encased arms rendered any movement difficult, hazardous, clumsy. The ride was stifling. The speakers played old songs. The driver hummed *Lovemepleaseloooveme*, laboring on the high notes. Behind me, a teenager was watching a sitcom without headphones. A family was eating triangular sandwiches. I wiped the window with my sleeve to clear a skylight and started to count green cars. At that early hour, there weren't very many, so I let myself be lulled by the bus's drone and my eyelids closed. Suddenly, a Spanish man yelled something in Spanish: we had arrived at the airport.

A hangar. Incredulous, I rubbed my eyes, but it was indeed a rectangular structure made from sheet metal. The slightest gust of wind could have overturned it. Nothing like the airport where we had set off for Fa'a'ā. Here, no glass wall or sculpture to amuse the eye. The carnival of rolling suitcases began. Their vibrant colors sharply contrasted with the surrounding grayness. I was disoriented.

Inside, two lines had formed: the priority passengers and those like me, who hadn't wanted to spend money on anything other than their spot. The employees smiled at those in the first line, said hello. For the rest of us, nada. This time, no special favors — my stomach was glued to the butt cheeks of the person in front of me. As if we were waiting for something important. But on the other side was only another waiting room.

Once at the security checkpoint, I held out my passport to the airport employee. The man in a white shirt and badge asked me if I was traveling alone.

'With my boyfriend.'

'Has he already gone through security?'

'No, he's in my pocket.'

The man laughed and wished me a good flight. I grabbed a plastic tray. Remove your shoes, belt, jewelry, anything that might set off the metal detector, except for pacemakers. Then more waiting: the plane wasn't ready. I bought a cereal bar from the vending machine and sat down on the ground because all the seats were taken. A janitor was washing the floor with clean water. My pants received a few splatters.

Economy turned out to be much less comfortable than I had imagined. Neck stooped. Back contorted. Legs folded. I would probably have been more comfortable in the cargo hold, wedged between a suitcase and a dog crate. To make matters worse, I'd been having chest pain since the day before.

To my left, the window looked out over the wing and the jet engine, which was so big that I could have traveled inside of it. On the tarmac, an employee in a bright orange vest was waving two fluorescent sticks. To my right, a woman had fallen asleep before takeoff. Too bad, she was going to miss the safety instructions. During my first flight, in first class, I was already drunk from champagne by this point and hadn't heard them. I identified the emergency exits. The flight attendant's gestures reminded me of my own at the studio. Was she paid a fair wage for this choreography? This is what to do if the cabin depressurizes, if a wing falls off, if we do a loop-the-loop, if we crash in the middle of the ocean. Don't forget to take off your high heels if we have to exit via the inflatable slide! A kind of comic strip had been stuck to the back of the seats. I studied it carefully. The little characters seemed extremely calm, considering the cockpit was on fire. I was impressed by their ironclad stoicism. Just before takeoff, I received a text from Sophie: she had passed. Bravo! Six years of higher education to get paid just over minimum wage and be insulted by kids all day long. Are we supposed to pop champagne for that? I sent an applause emoji along with 'Do you plan to pay me back for the hours of academic and psychological support?' She took it as a joke. Good for her.

The plane accelerated straight ahead and then bye bye gravity. First the nose, then the rear. I felt a commotion in my gut, but it wasn't so unpleasant. My ears clogged. We passed through a blind spot, then over the clouds. Cotton as far as the eye could see. I enjoyed imagining it as a rebirth.

A flight attendant came down the aisle with a large cart. He offered drinks, but also lottery tickets and duty-free perfume. No one bought a thing; the bottles stayed in their packaging. Just a few moments later, we had begun our descent.

From the sky, Ireland didn't look like much. Or, rather, it looked like all countries do from above: green and brown, a few hilly areas, and large grids of farm fields. The seatbelt symbol was illuminated; time to buckle up. My ears popped suddenly, and I slid a finger inside one to make sure I wasn't bleeding. Despite some turbulence, the plane continued straight. The asphalt drew closer and closer until the wheels touched down, bounced once or twice, and then slid down the runway. When the engine switched off, the older passengers applauded, as if to say thank you for not killing us. I found it sweet.

SELF-WORTH

The Dublin airport resembled the one I had been in a few hours prior, except for the signs in English. At the exit, I had to take a shuttle to the city center. Rain softened the ground, and mud smeared my suede boots. I had printed out the hotel address and a map of the city, which I had stored in a plastic pouch. Throughout the drive, I kept feeling the inside pocket of my jacket to make sure it was still in place. I got out of the car on a large avenue full of noise and people. Urban effervescence of horns and tailpipes. I walked for a little while, in water that formed little streams between the cobblestones. Brick walls. Red city. I found the hotel. Wiped my feet on the welcome mat. The receptionist spoke with a very distinct accent.

'No visitors allowed, okay?'

'Yes.'

'By visitors, I mean no men allowed, okay?'

'Yes.'

'One room, one person, okay?'

'Yes.'

Finally, he gave me the keys. The stairs were as steep as a climbing wall — you had to hike your thighs up to your shoulders to scale the steps — but eventually I arrived at my room. Minuscule. You couldn't open the door fully because the bed was in the way. There was no closet or shower, the communal bathroom was at the end of the hallway. The floral wallpaper resembled the pattern of the worn quilt, and, in the left corner of the room, a chair and bedside lamp completed the ensemble. Eighty-nine euros a night. Inflation, I guess.

I peeled myself like an onion. Layer after layer, the clothes gave way to my skin, my silhouette returned. I observed my body with some surprise. My thighs seemed less firm: I had aged. I looked out the window at the street, the bars, and the few tourists who were walking around despite the bad weather. I waited several minutes for the rain to stop, before realizing that it wasn't going to stop. My stomach gurgled threateningly. I put a sweater back on and left.

I rushed into the first open restaurant and ordered a stew, which was vile but a regional specialty. Pieces of unidentifiable meat swam in a brown sauce whose surface swelled with little grease bubbles, as if trying to escape. Potatoes and carrots hand in hand, united in this culinary catastrophe. When the waiter brought me the bill, I asked him if he had seen Lulu, showing him my phone. The photo was a little blurry because Lulu could never stop moving. The guy murmured something then cleared the table without even glancing at me.

I stayed seated at the wooden booth for an hour. I crumbled some bread, trying to follow the conversations of the regulars around me, but they were speaking too fast. On the television was a Gaelic football match, a startling blend of traditional soccer and rugby. The players tried to reach a goal, and could move the ball with their foot or their hand.

SELF-WORTH

Lulu would have found it amusing.

Once outside, I walked to St. Patrick's Cathedral. Sun peeked through the gray sky. Before I left, in order to identify places where I might find Lulu, I had typed in the search engine: 'What to do in Dublin?' In Rome, Paris, and London, dozens and dozens of historical buildings seemed to compete for our attention. Here, on the other hand, the websites listed only twelve 'must-see' destinations, including the cemetery. Apparently, the gothic architecture of St. Patrick's made it look like a haunted house. Standing out front, I tried to push open the heavy door. I felt resistance, so I pushed harder and then remembered Marc's advice from my first day at work: a door is made to be knocked down. Then a man slid his neck through the opening and yelled at me. I didn't understand if it was closed for service or construction. I showed the photo to him, too. He murmured his own unintelligible phrase.

I lingered in the park surrounding the cathedral. The green was very green; some birds I didn't recognize flew from one bench to another. I thought of Vladimir, whom I missed. I hoped that one day he would chirp as he used to. The humidity had lifted the paint from the bench, and I continued the work with my nail. I liked to see the wood reveal itself, as if I were helping it to breathe. Deep down, I was starting to despair. I was cold and dreaming of a latte macchiato. This city had none. Who wanted to live in such a nightmare? My psychological state was deteriorating.

Marc's phone number appeared on my screen. Shit, I had completely forgotten that I was an adult woman with super annoying obligations like showing up to work every morning.

'I'm so sorry, Marc, I'm unwell, I have to stay home.'

'Again? What do you have this time?'

'Pneumonia.'

I coughed to lend my story credibility.

'Pneumonia? Oh, Anna, I'm sorry ...'

Maybe pneumonia was a bit excessive. I tried to walk it back.

'Just a minor case of pneumonia. Don't worry, by next week I'll be back on my feet.'

'Do you think I'm an idiot? Do you have a doctor's note for this sick leave?'

'A what?'

'Anna, when you're sick, you need a doctor's note. Don't you know that? What world do you live in?'

I had been backed into a corner. Now I had to find a doctor to attest that I'd had an express pneumonia for seven days. Instead of thinking about it, I headed for the second cathedral on the list, Christ Church.

At the entrance, a large panel detailed the year of the building's construction, its particularities, and important facts to help understand the complexity of the building's history. This was repeated in every European language. I was open to learning, but the font size was microscopic, so

SELF-WORTH

I gave up. A woman appeared in front of me like an angel. I immediately proffered the photo of Lulu. She seemed sad for me and, to show it, shook her head from right to left. She tried to explain something to me. My technique of nodding my chin, smiling, and repeating 'Yes' didn't work. So, she grabbed my hand and brought me to a headset connected to the wall by a long cable. She handed it to me. 'No money, I have no money.' Even so, she planted the headphones on my head and left. In my ears: Handel. I didn't recognize it, I read it on a panel. It was beautiful. The kind of music you play at weddings or funerals. It suited the ambiance of the church; I was completely transported. I felt taller, pulled by a string attached to the top of my head towards the ceiling of the nave. A string that lifted me up, not like the one at work that turned me into a puppet. The violins seemed to caress the statues. My body warmed up enough that I could stop rubbing my hands together.

At the end of the song, the woman returned. Once again, she extended her arm, and I let her guide me. We went down into the crypt. Medieval armor of all varieties was displayed in glass cases. The knights, the épées, the folklore — I wasn't really interested in that stuff. But I didn't want to seem ungrateful, so I resumed my chin nods as I listened to her explanations.

Suddenly, her mouth twisted into a cheerful grin. She must have been showing me the centerpiece of the church, the crown jewel, perhaps even the most valuable treasure in the entire country. Her fingers flapped in the air and betrayed her impatience. I was expecting to find the tomb of some saint that I probably wouldn't know. But her excitement was contagious, and I started to get excited too.

We stopped in front of a tiny display case pushed into a corner. The woman was right to make such a fuss. I was surprised. Inside was a cat chasing a rat. A panel explained that the cadavers were authentic. They had been found mummified due to the lack of air in the organ pipe. I found it a really beautiful metaphor, but for what, I wasn't sure. I was blown away. It was incredibly well preserved, the cat still had its whiskers, the scene looked alive. A medieval episode of *Tom and Jerry*, frozen for all eternity.

Before leaving the church, I slid a few coins into the donation box. I probably needed the money more than the Catholic institution, but I sensed it would please the woman. I lit a candle and prayed. I asked God (whether he be perfect, dead, or even a double-pincer lobster) to help me find Lulu and to make me rich again.

Outside, the rain had resumed. I got lost along the roads, I found wandering quite pleasant. The more I concentrated on my footsteps, the more immediate my thoughts became. Melancholy pierced through only intermittently.

By chance, I ran into Oscar Wilde. The writer was sitting on a rock, in a rather incongruous pose. He seemed affectedly relaxed, one leg extended sensually, while his face expressed great suffering. He gripped the stone with his right hand in order to postpone the inevitable fall. For more realism, the statue had been painted. Green cardigan and gray pants, the local style, slightly old-fashioned. I spent the rest of the day crossing off the various places on my list. I asked about fifty people. Lulu was nowhere to be found.

In Ireland, there are three sources of national pride: Beckett, Joyce, and Guinness. Even Wilde comes after these. The first, I knew well. The second, I didn't understand at all. So I settled for the third.

Night had fallen early. Under the gleam of streetlights, the red of bricks gave way to charcoal-gray walls. A city drawn on paper with crayon. Scribbled metropolis. I went back up the street to reach the center. There, I had plenty of choices. Temple Bar and other pubs at every intersection. One of them was called The Lost Souls. The interior was visible behind the foggy glass of the façade, and it seemed nice and warm inside. I sat at a high table in the shape of a barrel. I counted the coins I had left. The backpacker's guide had been clear: the cost of living in Dublin was quite high. Even so, I ordered a pint. I hoped that the hops would dissolve the lump in my throat.

I was quickly accosted by a young man. The look of a typical Irishman. Angelic flush on skin flecked with gold. Crooked teeth behind fine lips. Cherubic face juxtaposed with a massive body. Probably a Gaelic football player. Large shoulders. Confident stride.

'Are you okay? You look sad.'
'Yes.'
'Are you alone in Dublin?'
'Yes, I'm a widow.'
'You're French, right? You have that French cynicism.'

Connor, he told me. I wasn't in the mood to chat. I watched him walk over with his large shoes and zero finesse. I would have to simper, pretend. I wanted to cut the conversation short, but the boy didn't. He ordered two more beers. Nothing about our chat was interesting. Connor was studying global marketing and dreamed of living in Paris, which he had never visited. He painted a picture of a fanciful city. A variation on *Amélie*, without the accordion. He spoke of the splendor of the architecture, the romanticism, the sense of style, while I stared at his holey sweater and worn sneakers. 'Not now, but soon,' he fantasized. Out of spite, I was tempted to mention the hundreds of rats, the tents under the bridges, and the crackheads in the metro, but I didn't feel like being a bitch. Illusions help people sleep at night.

Connor politely asked about me. I told him that I lived in the triangle d'or, in a humble apartment with a fireplace and a balcony.

'What? How did you get so much money? You must have a super impressive job!'

Therein lies the rub. As I had with Veronica, so as not to lose face, I started to make things up. Completely. A delirium so believable that I convinced myself. This time, I was the producer of a TV show in Paris. I decided on the content and rubbed shoulders with important people who wore suits and carried briefcases. I spent my time in the air, aboard a private jet belonging to the production company. It was an exhausting job. Then I told him loads of stories about international celebrities that I'd heard at the studio. I appropriated them, emphasizing my proximity to 'the elite'. The words came out on their own, effortlessly. With a disconcerting ease.

'You have a beautiful voice. And such a nice laugh,' he gushed.

I gave Connor what he wanted. He drank up every last word, even the gobs of spit. His chest leaned forward as if to shorten the distance between my words and his ears. He was gripping the table with both hands, punctuating my tales with 'No! Seriously?' When I ran out of ideas, I headed for the bathroom to buy myself time to invent something new.

When I came back, the room had filled up. Men mostly, already drunk. They must have been making the rounds of the bars. I almost had to climb over them to reach our table again. Connor pulled me out of the human flood. We ordered more drinks at the bar. I liked the contrast between the white foam and the dark amber of the beer. The bartender put on 'Angie' and all the drunkards started to sing. They stood arm in arm. I was caught up in their movement. We were squeezed in so tightly that my feet lifted from the floor. Beer spilled on my coat, but it didn't matter. I was having fun, jostled in every direction. The lump in my throat bounced around, top to bottom and left to right, like a pinball machine. I wanted it to last forever. I yelled the words to the song in unison with the others.

Connor brought me back down brusquely. When the music stopped, he lifted his shirt to show me his abs. 'Your hotel?' he asked, trying to be suave. I glanced at his torso, hoping to see the same marks as on Lulu. Zero. Smooth as a baby's butt. I said I needed a cigarette and scrammed.

It was drizzling again, lighter now. I spun around to head back to the local bus stop, which was opposite a sign that promised a 'Joycean adventure'. Waiting for the bus, I wondered whether the experience included a perforated duodenal ulcer. Seated next to me, a small group of girls were talking loudly and playing with each other's hair. Dressed in skirts too short for the season, their faces falsely tanned with makeup. I shivered as I listened to their conversation. One of them couldn't decide whether to sleep with a guy named Ian. They went to the top floor of the bus; I followed them. Zippers. Mascara. Eyeshadow. Comb. Perfume. Laughs like in kindergarten. The smell of strawberry Tagadas wafted throughout the bus. I envied them because they were floating in the certainty that at the end of this bus line, something fantastic awaited them, better than a Connor, Ian, or any other Irish name combined. The night, perhaps even that very night, which for them was just beginning, opened the doors to a necessarily bright future. An absolute confidence gleamed in their eyes. What did they see in mine? Nothing: they weren't paying any attention to me. The nocturnal group I was a part of served only as secondary characters in a world that revolved around them, was made for them, and waited only for them to blossom. Their naiveté was precious. Let them enjoy it now; the hangover would catch up to them soon enough.

I entered the hotel lobby. Wiped my shoes on the welcome mat. The receptionist looked behind me to make sure I was alone. After climbing to my floor, I hit the door against the bed. He coughed with an air of reproach. Down below, he could apparently hear everything. I tried to turn on the light, in vain. So I lay down fully dressed, swaddled in my coat and gloves because it was so cold. Above me, a couple was having sex. The lump emerged from my body, took up all the space in the room and then finally lay down next to me.

I woke up early the next day. I thought I heard a woman snickering, but it was just the wind sweeping through the old alleyways. The soundtrack of a horror movie. Maybe it wasn't the ideal day, but oh well, I had no choice: there was just one place left on my list.

After a breakfast of very black coffee, I grabbed my backpack and said goodbye to the receptionist. I donned my beanie and took off along the quays. My hair whipped violently around my face. My hands were as dry as parchment.

The docks looked very different from the historical center. An old privateer ship seemed to have washed up in the middle of ultramodern construction. Glass towers gleaming silver. Iron and concrete soaring high into the heavy sky. The water of the Liffey was brown with a purplish tint, a vein dividing the city. I tried to make out what was beneath the surface, but the water was too murky. It probably concealed plastic bags, maybe the frames of stolen cars. I walked more slowly than the current; the wind was blowing against me. Dozens of gulls danced in procession. They traced concentric circles that got smaller and smaller and then, suddenly, nosedived. Others, lazier, settled for ripping open trash.

Eventually, I reached the Samuel Beckett Bridge. It was a strange structure that actually resembled a large, dislocated gull. I wasn't convinced that Beckett would have liked it. I kept walking and stopped in the middle, at the place where the arch was at its peak. The wind stopped for a moment, as if the universe was, for once, showing me a sign of respect. I rubbed the bill from Lulu that I had kept as a good luck token between my hands, caressing one final time the ersatz of his body that I had touched so often.

SELF-WORTH

The place was deserted. I cried 'Lulu, Lulu, Luluuuuuuuu,' hoping that my voice would reach into all the pubs and apartments of this cursed city. The sound flew away and then fell back down, leaving nothing but silence. I crossed the bridge in one direction and then the other. At one point, I thought I felt a hand on my shoulder. I turned around: there was no one but me. I sat down and waited for Lulu turned Godot. For hours, it seemed. A woman pushing a child in a stroller approached me. She bent down and slid something into my hand: a two-euro coin. This was the final straw. Lulu, the love of my life, wasn't coming back for me. I used the coin to scratch words into the bridge: 'My beloved, come back to Paris. I'll love you forever even if you stop growing money out of your back.' I took the bill from my pocket and threw it into the water. I watched it twirl for a moment, a paper butterfly, and land delicately on the dark mass. It drifted along with the flow of the river, then disappeared.

In my remaining hours, I went in search of souvenirs. Kitsch galore in green and orange, snow globes and lighters that would only work once. I felt the urge to load up my arms. I happened upon a small store lined with tchotchkes from floor to ceiling. Some suddenly lit up when you passed by. Stuffed St. Patrick dolls sang as soon as they detected someone. Good thing I didn't have epilepsy or a heart condition. Behind the counter, the other side of the Channel's version of Christelle. Same attitude of 'don't try to pull one over on me', same determined gum chewing. An ashtray in the shape of a four-leaf clover and a beer mug with the inscription 'Dublin is always a good idea' caught my eye. Irish Christelle stared at me indifferently through a funny rearview mirror tucked behind the cash register to make sure I wasn't stealing anything. As I approached, I gave her a big smile, which she did not return. I entered my pin: card declined. My arms would remain full of emptiness.

13

All the doctors' clinics I called to get a note about my pneumonia hung up on me. That is, when they didn't insult me savagely. I returned to work with my tail between my legs. Of course, I didn't expect a welcome wagon, but I was still caught off guard when Marc started to yell at me as soon as he spotted my foot in the opening of that infamous door. Just then, Sandrine, who never missed a beat, brought him a cinnamon roll and a chai latte, and he calmed down.

Thierry did my head in again talking about pita bread and white sauce. He thought it was ironclad, the perfect solution for me. Had Lulu gone back to work?

'I got dumped, Thierry, just forget about it.'

'Ah, that's guys for you. They take you, use you, and then throw you out like an old sock as soon as they have a little dough. Me though, I'm not like that ...'

I recoiled when he tried to rub my shoulder. But then I

realized that, in my situation, I had no other choice than to play the game.

'Actually, I'm glad you're here. I'm having some trouble making ends meet, do you think you could spot me some rent money? I'm already behind, and I'm worried about ending up on the street.'

As I spoke, I twirled a strand of hair with my index finger and tried to give him sexy-piercing-sweet-desperate glances. Thierry stiffened.

'You're not paying your rent anymore? Do you realize that puts me in deep shit with my friend? I vouched for you, I said you could be trusted. Honestly, Anna, quit messing around. I'm retiring soon. A peaceful life, is that so much to ask? I won't rat you out, but I won't cover for you either. From now on, we don't know each other. Thierry? Never heard of him, an old acquaintance from work who disappeared one day. Understood? As for cash, I've got zilch.'

Thus concluded our speculative friendship of a few weeks. I could only count on myself now.

The audience entered. We did a couple of tests, to make sure I hadn't lost my touch. Marc wasn't happy: 'Pay attention, good grief, are you kidding me, is your hand deformed or what? You need to go to an ENT, you're off balance.' I was tempted to rip out his artery, but it was possible I already had one murder to my name: no use making things worse. I raised my hands quickly. They laughed. The men and women became creatures. No longer anything but tongues, glottises, vocal cords. I couldn't see the rest of their faces. Swallowed up by those mouths, ever more voracious. At the sound of the four notes of the theme song, the show began. The lighting had been modified at the request of Bertrand, who complained that it accentuated his wrinkles. I worked zealously, hoping Marc would notice. At the break, I summoned my courage.

'I need a raise.'

'Dream on, doll! You're already on the chopping block after your fake pneumonia story and you have the nerve to ask for more money?'

'It's for my rent, my groceries … it's a precarious situation, I'm struggling.'

He offered me extra hours, even though I didn't deserve it, but fine, he wasn't about to let a colleague crash and burn. I took them all, showing up even when there was nothing to do. But it still wasn't enough.

Each night, in front of my door, I found envelopes. All the same. White, rectangular. My name and address visible through the small plastic window. Impersonal. Letterhead with the ominous logo: République française, or EDF/GDF. Cold sweat. Fingers trembling. How much this time? The metro turnstile that doesn't turn anymore. Expired subscription. Call. Green number. Possibility of deferring payment? No, mademoiselle, if we make an exception for you, we'd have to do it for everybody. What about a Vélib', have you thought of that? Yes, but it takes me over an hour on public transport, so on a bike, you can imagine how long it would take. I understand, but it's more environmentally friendly and more economical.

Bank account in the red, redder and redder, verging on scarlet. The negative written in gray. Days that dragged on: the end of the month seemed always further away. At the end of a long tunnel. Is it only the twelfth? A warning. Then a second. In deeper, deeper. The salary that barely plugged the hole. Another crack formed, and with it the risk of falling in. The envelopes hounded me even in the mugginess of sleep. I opened the door and hundreds of bills cascaded to land in the middle of the living room. The pile climbed dangerously high, to the point of suffocation. We have the nightmares of our class.

At the peak of my despair, I called Marjorie. She was stunned. Any particular problem? No. I just want to earn more money. I asked if it was possible to interview for another job, on top of the one she had previously found for me. Marjorie snickered: 'It's perfectly feasible to get by on minimum wage, you're already lucky. The employment office can no longer help you at this stage. And besides, holding two CDIs at the same time is impossible, you have to sleep after all, get some rest. "Sleep is the only free gift the Gods bestow."' Plutarch: touché. Nothing else to say.

She insisted: 'Anna, you seem very stressed, are you sure everything's okay?' I faked a laugh and hung up.

The next morning, I received a visit from two not-so-friendly guys. They pounded on the door so hard that I thought it was a police raid. It was worse.

'You not pay rent. You pay now. Or else — *scouik*.'

Looking back, I'm probably exaggerating the Russian accent, but in the moment, my heart was in my throat. Even so, the word 'scouik' made me crack a smile, despite those men's biceps and scarred faces. Then they took out a knife that seemed big enough to impale a human and spun it around like a kebab spit. A sweet thought for Thierry. My smile vanished. One of the two slapped the back of my head so that the threat would embed itself in my skull. A little dazed, I watched them walk down the street. They were arguing, gesturing wildly and, this time, it was the second guy who slapped the neck of the other. It must have been tradition. They hopped on their Vélib's. Turning onto the boulevard, they indicated with their left arms, so as not to be hit by a car. Message received: I had to get out of there asap.

I called Sophie. 'Hey, how's it going, it's been a while, of course I want to hear about your life!' I hoped she wouldn't talk about *Befindlichkeit* or some other tedious theory. But Sophie wasn't in the mood to philosophize. She had passed the CAPES, but things weren't turning out as she had hoped. She had pictured herself in *Dead Poets Society*, students standing on their desks railing against Cicero's speeches, but had found herself faced with a band of teens who, obviously, didn't give a fuck about the difference between nature versus nurture. Bristol pads had given way to mass-produced copies. Red again, red everywhere. They understood nothing, she complained.

'And on top of that, my landlord is driving me nuts, I have to find a new apartment.'

Perfect timing. I didn't even have to insist.

'Me too, Sophie. We could live together, what do you think?'

'What about that amazing apartment from Lulu's uncle?'

'We broke up. Well ... he left me.'

'Oh my God! I'm so full of myself, I've been going on and on about my problems while you're really struggling right now. I know how hard it is ...'

No, she didn't know. The only relationship Sophie had been in was a one-sided obsession with an expert in analytical philosophy. An old man with a faded blue three-piece suit and a very pronounced eye twitch. At the end of his seminars on Wittgenstein, which she attended religiously, she would always ask a heap of questions. He'd reply with a lisp that she had understood nothing of the *Tractatus Logico-Philosophicus*. Sophie must have been a bit of a masochist, because she would re-enter the fray each week, while most students deserted the course after day one. She waited for the end of the semester to declare her love for him, and he replied with something nonsensical: 'Whereof one cannot speak thereof one must be silent,' from the same austere Wittgenstein text. Rather than feeling rejected, the poor thing had interpreted this as a mystical revelation and proceeded to slip notes into his mailbox for months — until he registered a complaint with the police. And thus, her idyll came to an end. I needed her to move in with me, so I said:

'Girlfriends are all that matters. We'll throw incredible pajama parties!'

I bit my tongue saying those words.

'For sure! I'll start looking now.'

Obviously, our apartment was in a two-digit arrondissement. Given its distance from the city center, it merited a third. The only benefit was that it was closer to the studio. Sophie had shown me places in the suburbs. She used expressions like 'it's charming', 'a small village', 'you feel a world away from Paris'. I categorically refused. What would be next? The provinces? Out of the question. Luckily, Sophie was malleable by nature, and since we were going to live together, each of us would have to make concessions. Okay, she agreed, we'll stay in the city.

A one-bedroom. No balcony or fireplace. Instead of moldings, the walls bore the traces of the thumbtacks used to display the shitty posters of the previous tenants. But Sophie was delighted. She waited for the end of the tour to show me the best part: a heated towel rack in the bathroom. So great, right? A golden opportunity: the landlord was happy to rent to two serious employed young women. I signed without even glancing at the lease. I was too depressed.

We emptied my old apartment quickly. Unplugged all the electrical appliances and carried out the furniture and various objects. Since they wouldn't all fit in our new place, I had to make choices. We abandoned a great deal on the sidewalk. The July sun lit up Sophie's hair, giving her an angelic glow as she jumped on top of boxes to flatten them. I imagined the RATP security guards intrigued and then bursting into laughter watching our multiple back-and-forths on the metro, first with a floor lamp, thirty minutes later with a stereo. The living room was transformed into a bedroom so that we could each have our own space. We just had to repatriate the fridge. Sandrine gave us a hand. Her back was aching, and she couldn't carry anything too heavy, so she swept the floor, folded up some clothes. When she stooped down to collect the dust, I noticed that her tailbone was bruised. I thought maybe this was the right time to broach a conversation, away from the studio and the peer pressure.

'Oh, it looks like you really hurt yourself.'

Terrified expression. She lowered her T-shirt and pulled

her pants back up to hide the area.

'I wasn't hit or anything, it's just that I ...'

'Fell down the stairs?'

She looked at the floor, but the small heap of dust couldn't save her.

'That's it, yes, the stairs. I must polish them too much or something.'

Sophie, ever the space cadet, suggested:

'I have these amazing non-slip socks. If you want, I can give them to you!'

'And your boyfriend, how's it going, is he making any money on sports betting?' I pressed.

Sandrine's eyes began to water.

'No, not really ... That's why things are a little complicated right now. But it's fine, really, it'll pass.'

'We're here, if you ever need to ...'

'What's that smell?' Sophie interrupted.

She crouched down in front of the fridge. Before I could warn her, she let out a horrified scream. Opening the freezer door, she found Estragon, who had thawed. She was now holding him by her fingertips, his eyes like marbles, and waving him under my nose to demand an explanation. I covered Vladimir's cage with my arms so as not to trigger any post-traumatic stress. We decided to throw the dead bird in the communal trash.

Once we were settled in, Sophie wanted to throw a housewarming party. I told her that I didn't want the people in my life seeing the downward spiral I was in. 'What spiral? What do you mean downward?' asked Sophie. 'Our life is super cool!' At the very least, she wanted to invite Mehdi over, he'd been our friend forever. He would never come.

'Just because you're a materialistic asshole doesn't mean he won't be able to forgive you.'

Thanks for that lovely optimism. When I still resisted, she made a new concession: no housewarming, but every night we would have the promised pajama party. Sophie was wearing a gigantic onesie with fake fur bunny ears. We put on face masks while watching a reality TV show where a group of morons argued over every little thing. I envied those morons. I would have given anything to be in a villa paid to do absolutely nothing. I dreamed of arguing over a slice of bread or who was sleeping with whom. Sophie, on the other hand, criticized their poor decisions and incessant fighting. Even so, she obsessively followed their love affairs and knew the names of all the contestants.

One night, while we were slumped on her bed, the doorbell rang. I had begged Sophie not to give our address to anyone. The two pseudo-Russians popped into my head. She said she hadn't, she didn't know who it could be. Vladimir emitted a worried cluck tinged with excitement. I grabbed the biggest knife we had from the kitchen. The doorbell kept ringing. I pulled open the door and Sandrine appeared. Face swollen, lip bleeding, brow cut open. She threw herself into my arms.

SELF-WORTH

'This time, I'm leaving. I've made up my mind. I thought he was going to kill me. Can I stay with you?'

And that's how Sandrine I-ran-into-the-door, Sandrine I-fell-down-the-stairs, Sandrine I-hit-myself-on-the-cabinet, Sandrine it's-nothing-just-a-bruise, Sandrine the scatterbrain left her apartment and her boyfriend. We bandaged her wounds for a few days. She gradually recovered her cheery disposition. The rent was now split three ways, which helped to repay the debts I had accumulated at various agencies and boutiques. For lack of space, Sandrine slept in my bed, and I have to admit that her presence allowed me to fill Lulu's absence. I still thought of him from time to time, and immediately my chest would begin to hurt, an unbearable pain.

Whenever we talked late into the night, I finally felt like I had real friends. The proof: I sold one of my last Fendi bags so that I could give Sophie a deluxe edition of Pascal's *Pensées* for her birthday, a hardcover volume with gilt edging and glossy paper. She was genuinely moved; her fingers trembled as she turned the pages. I felt a twinge in my chest; I checked my pulse. Surprise! I had a heart. I was almost happy. Almost.

14

I soon grew tired of the pajama parties. Once you've tasted caviar, tuna becomes inedible. I relapsed often, each time more violently than the last. A pressure on my sternum, the lump in my throat turned to lead. I couldn't take it anymore.

For the last three weeks, I'd been cruising all the trendy nightclubs. On the prowl. Lying in wait. I kept vigil late into the night and went home in the early morning. The girls asked, 'Hey, already up?' and I answered with a groan. Just enough time to wipe away the traces of mascara streaming down my cheeks and swap the sequin dress for a more understated outfit. I slept on the RER. At work too, more and more often.

In the savannah, it's the lioness who hunts. Nostrils dilated. Muzzle up in the air. I liked the scent of those dark rooms, a hint of sweat and vodka pomme spilled on the floor. Call it what you like — cash, bucks, loot, bacon, dough, bread, or moolah — money always has the same smell. Delicate. Cotton fibers covered in a layer of protective coating. Sometimes, a bitter fragrance of light grime. Unmistakable.

Bodies graze each other in those spaces, deliberately overcrowded. We go to beg for human, carnal contact. Skin on skin, like infants. Speakers turned up to max. At the limit of the human ear's tolerance threshold. You can't hear each other, and it doesn't matter: no one is there to talk.

Often, I only found losers there on a Saturday night, who, stuffing bills into the dancers' bikinis, believed they were taking their revenge on life. That didn't interest me. I was looking for the jackpot.

That Wednesday, I saw him straight away. Even from afar. In the middle of that absurd galaxy, I saw him straight away. He became the center. Beautiful as the sun. A white face framed by jet-black hair. High cheekbones beneath eyes whose color I couldn't make out from a distance. But I recognized him by the way his chest was itching. He scratched his white shirt with a very specific vigor. There was no doubt about it.

The lioness in me awakened. Sniff out my prey. Watch him. Lie low then leap at the opportune moment. Lift my hair. Sway from side to side. Rock my pelvis right to left and left to right. To the rhythm of the music. Step by step to the techno. Careful. Don't let him out of your sight. Tonight, you're mine. Mouth slightly open. Eyelids batting. Sensual. Approach him. Ensnare him. Leave him no choice. Hand grasps hip. Palm caresses cheek. He tried to tell me his name. I placed a finger on his wet lips.

'Who cares? Don't ruin the moment.'

Voice like Fanny Ardant. This stretched the fabric of his jeans. A bulge. Quickly, accept a drink. A few dances to keep up the act. I tried to lift his shirt.

'You're bold. I like that.'

But he immediately lowered it, tugging on the hem. Through the thin fabric I could make out violet markings: five-hundred-euro bills. Bingo. Grin from ear to ear. Lips curled up, drool at the corners. Lioness turned hyena.

A taxi hurtled towards us. His body next to mine on the leather seat. I charged again. Delicate caress. Tongues. In the rearview mirror, I caught the glances of the driver, who couldn't stop himself from watching us. Utterly shameless, I undid the first button of my prey's shirt, then the second.

'You're tickling me. Not here, let's wait until we're at the apartment.'

But I needed to smell the scent, so I kept up my ruse by sticking my nose on his neck and continuing to open his shirt. The driver turned off the interior light. I could see the markings, feel the ridges.

'You're scratching me, that hurts! Stop, please.'

I was deaf to his cries. My fingers were furrowing faster and deeper. I needed to tear that skin. Reach the marrow, the cash. I used my teeth. I bit too hard. My canines pierced through; warm liquid poured into my mouth. I felt his cartilage crackle like the top of a crème brûlée. Instinctively, he slapped me. The driver slowed down.

'Hey! Are you crazy? If you're on some kind of BDSM trip, that's not my thing. I can't believe this. Get out of the car, right now.'

'I'm sorry, but those spots on your torso, I was …'

'Yeah, I have eczema, so what? It's much more common than people think. There's nothing to be ashamed of, I'm a little stressed, that's all. Why am I explaining this to you? I don't have to justify myself. Get out of here, you psycho!'

He pushed me outside. I was so stunned, I didn't react. I slid from the back seat and found myself on the ground, the cold asphalt under my legs. The stranger slammed the door, and the taxi continued its path through Paris.

15

I needed some warmth. My entire body was shivering. I found one of Lulu's sweatshirts that, by some miracle, had survived the move. I nestled myself inside it and slept until dreams seemed as concrete as reality. I was sweating, my fever rising. I didn't wake up until Sophie or Sandrine, worried, came to check whether I was still alive. At the end of my long coma, I went to take a shower.

The bathroom mirror reflected a strange face. I stretched it in every direction as if it belonged to someone else but no, there was no one underneath but me. How could someone change so rapidly? The brown roots of my hair were visible under the platinum blonde. The natural was chasing away the artifice — the horror! Hair unbrushed and no makeup on, I looked once more like my fourteen-year-old self, which is to say like nobody. Two bulging eyes on a sad face.

I took off my sweatpants and then my sweater. That's when they appeared. The outlines of pronounced grooves. Rectangular, reassuring. A work of art, à la Mondrian. I approached the mirror to inspect further. The bills were right there, under my skin. I could see them, smell them. My body was finally emitting the bitter fragrance I had coveted for so long. The sweatshirt had contaminated me. A huge smile lifted my cheeks. I scratched scratched scratched. My nails turned red. Blood spilled onto the Ikea rug. But I grabbed hold of nothing. I had to dig into my flesh, my hands weren't strong enough. I ran to the kitchen. Butcher knife. Cake slicer. An abundance of choice. I noticed the peeler, drying peacefully at the edge of the sink. I grabbed it like a lifeline and, back in the bathroom, I scraped, skinned, peeled. Shreds of skin came off in thick bloody strips before falling to the floor. I shoved a towel in my mouth to muffle my screams. I was excavating myself. Red vessels. White fat. My insides revealed the same conclusion as the surface: I was ugly. And now, I didn't have my father to comfort me with his crepes. Trembling, tendons convulsing, not used to being thus exposed. With my free hand, I grabbed onto the sink to keep from falling. My legs buckled; I was leaving my body. That's when Sophie slid her head through the door frame. She cried out just before I fainted.

16

Near the end of the recording, I felt a vibration in my pocket. My heart skipped a beat, then started racing. The vibration again. More and more intense. *Lulu*, I thought immediately. *He's coming back!* The buzzing continued. I confused gestures, told the audience to laugh when it wasn't appropriate. I refrained from grabbing my phone; if I did, Marc would get angry, we'd have another argument. The phone went quiet. Then another, different vibration: a text. Should I risk it? Just then came a lull. Bertrand talked talked talked, and he hated to be interrupted during his monologues, those were the five most important minutes of the show. He would announce the winner. Happy recipient of ten thousand euros, rewarded for their humor. The lucky contestant would make one final joke, and everyone would start to laugh again. A heavy silence took over the studio, all the cameras were aimed at the host. I went for it. I slid my fingers, tapped the screen. It was Sophie. Vladimir had fallen from his perch. He was dead. Then all the mouths began to spin around me, a macabre dance. A whirlwind of teeth, cavities, fillings. I crossed the camera's field of view to seek refuge near Sandrine. Amidst the jubilant crowd, I sobbed.

17

A woman is smiling at me. She's wearing scrubs, like a nurse. Everything about her is welcoming. Her arms are open, her white blouse is extremely clean, she seems silky and soft. Her skin is smooth, she appears well rested. No trace of dark circles under her eyes. Nothing seems to indicate that she is paid peanuts, that half of her salary goes to paying for gas and the nanny, that she goes home every night with the desire to defenestrate herself, and that her sole pleasure is in a Netflix series she consumes obsessively. Same for the poster next to it, a man in a bus driver uniform smiling wide enough to unhook his jaw because yes, it's wonderful to spend six hours a day driving a big bulky vehicle through Parisian bottlenecks, braving insults and the chewing gum stuck under the seats. The reflection of the light on the glossy paper blinds his gaze.

I grab a ticket. Number 92. I wait for my turn. The tile

grout has blackened since the last time I was here. There are some newcomers. Boys and girls, embarrassed but full of enthusiasm. They still smell like the waxed university benches. I notice Mehdi, sitting on a chair in the corner and carefully avoiding me as I wave, gaze lowered to his canvas sneakers. I get up to sit with him and talk, but he gives me the finger. I sit back down. I'm here to make the pilgrimage once more. I've been laid off. The rock fell from the mountain top, and I have to push it back up again. Perhaps one must imagine Sisyphus happy, but it's difficult.

Several numbers flit by on the bright screen. Never mine. There's a whole gaggle of us. A farandole of the poor. I receive a text from my father: 'Happy birthday, Anna! I sent you a hundred euros. The big two-five, that's something to celebrate!' Ah, here we go. They're calling number 92.

Acknowledgements

This book is for my mother, Catherine: I haven't forgotten you.s

Thank you to my father, Joël, for being someone I admire, for his guidance, and for his delicious cookies.

Thank you to Corentin, aka Coco, for his love and his unrivalled jokes.

Thank you to my family, the absolute best: Léa, Fredy, Étienne, Stéphane, and Mehdi.

Thank you to Camille Ancel, without whom this book would be at the bottom of my trash can.

Thank you to Anna Khachaturova for her work, her kindness, and her benevolence.

Thank you to Emma Ramadan, Marika Webb-Pullman, and the entire team of Scribe Publications for their great work and enthusiasm.

Thank you to Laure Salathé for supporting (and

tolerating) me.

Thank you to Anne-Ré, my lifelong accomplice.

Thank you to my friends for their encouragement.

Thank you to the Italians for inventing the margherita pizza.